The Positive Freedom Field Trip

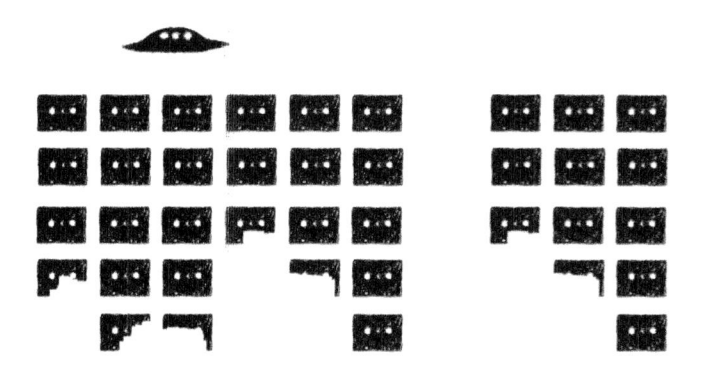

Lol Watson

The Positive Freedom Field Trip
Copyright © Lol Watson 2024

Lol Watson asserts his right under the Copyright, Designs and Patents Act 1988 to be identified as the author of this work.

All rights reserved. This includes the right to reproduce any portion of this book in any form.

This book is a work of fiction. The characters are fictitious and any resemblance to actual persons, living or dead, is purely coincidental.

ISBN 979-8-883-36319-0

Typeset – Libre Caslon Text (Google font).
Cover design by Lol Watson. Cover and artwork created using GIMP 2.10.
Cover and diagram typeset – Love Ya Like A Sister (Google font).
(Google fonts licensed under the SIL Open Font License, Version 1.1.)

For Helen, who looks after my soul.

Chapter 1

Passion. Why do people keep going on about passion? Every time you turn on the television there are people making claims like 'Food is my passion,' or, 'You have to have the passion to succeed.' You get all those cooking shows and reality programmes with the hosts and presenters screaming at everyone to 'Come on, show me a bit of passion!' What's all that about?

I've been shunted onto this line of thought by a letter that's just been posted through my letterbox. I'm reading this letter while sat at my desk, drinking a cup of coffee and nibbling on a Choco Leibniz biscuit (to my mind it's never too early in the day for a Choco Leibniz). The letter is from my internet provider, FastWeb (tagline: broadband the way you want it). 'Dear Mr Gunson,' it begins. 'As you know, customer service is our passion.' And then it goes on to talk about the new, improved service they would like to give me and how much I will benefit from having it and then they tell me how much extra money it's going to cost.

Passion.

Passion.

Passion.

It's strange, isn't it? Repeat a word too many times and it ends up becoming just a sound, alienated from its meaning. I can't help wondering though. Can a corporate entity like a telecom company be said to have a 'passion' for anything? Really?

You see, philosophers have a particular idea in mind when they use the word 'passion'. To them, a 'passion' is the opposite of an 'action'. Just in the way that 'active' is the opposite of 'passive'. So whereas an action is something that you do, something that you cause to happen, a passion is something that happens to you, something that you don't have any control over.

And, when talking about the things that people describe as their 'passions,' I think that this does make a certain amount of sense. If you say that you have a passion for something, are you not saying that the way you feel about it isn't entirely under your control? Because the passion controls you. You might even go so far as to say that the passion chooses you, rather than the other way round.

Of course, in the most typical sense of the word, a passion is something that you love. And when it comes to love, I think that what I said just now does seem to be true. Yes, in my experience at least, being in love or falling in love with someone has always been something that just happened to me, without my having very much say in the matter.

And here's another case to consider. I have a friend and colleague, Tim Brenner, who is one of the other teachers at the college where I work. Tim and I were doing a Zoom call just the other day, actually. We were supposed to be talking about how we were going to manage our classes, since the college is currently closed due to the national lockdown. But instead we ended up talking about football. Or, more specifically, I spent the call listening to Tim complaining about how all his important football fixtures have been cancelled for the foreseeable future.

Tim, I should tell you, is a life-long supporter of his local team, Cove Alexandra Football Club. He is a dedicated follower of that team. So dedicated, in fact, that he hardly ever misses a match. Home games, away games, weekends and week nights, any weather, any distance, he will go to every match they play. All the travelling this involves is expensive and time consuming, so he tells me, and in spite of all his support the team never seems to win much.

The rewards for all his efforts, in my opinion, have always appeared to be rather limited and I've told him this on several occasions. His response is usually to go on about how the times when they do win make up for all the times when they don't. I have occasionally suggested that, if he switched his allegiance to a team that won more games, then he might get a bit more value out of the experience. But he just shakes his head and tells me I don't understand anything about football.

So, like I said, during our Zoom call last week Tim was going on about how there was no football being played anywhere at the moment. As far as I could make out, he was really distraught about being denied the opportunity of watching his team suffer yet another humiliating defeat. I would therefore argue that the way Tim feels about Cove Alexandra Football Club can be described as a 'passion' in the philosopher's sense of the word. His desire to go and see them play isn't something he seems to have any control over. He doesn't even seem to enjoy it most of the time; it's just something that he feels compelled to do.

But of course most people aren't philosophers. And they don't think that way. Most people, when they say they have a 'passion' about something, what they mean is enthusiasm, ambition, drive, energy, things like that. That's what those TV chefs have in mind when they use the word. And doubtless that's what the FastWeb people mean when they tell me they have a passion for customer service. I'm sure FastWeb wouldn't want to say that the way they feel about customer service is something that just happens, something that they have no control over. Would they?

Anyway, FastWeb are offering me a faster internet speed but I think what I currently have is fast enough. I really ought to be testing this out by turning on my laptop and actually getting on with some work, instead of wasting my time wondering about the definitions of random words.

I sit back and watch the laptop chug through its start-up sequence while I reach for another Choco Leibniz biscuit. The laptop was supplied by the college and it isn't the speediest of machines. But, a few minutes later (and another couple of biscuits later) the email program is open and running. I watch the screen as it shows my inbox filling up with all the essays from my students, ready for me to go through and mark. As I said, it's not super-quick but it seems to be working okay and running well enough for me. So thanks for the offer, FastWeb, but I don't think I'm in any immediate need of your more expensive service just now.

These essays are from a new set of students. A new tutorial group. Ordinarily I would have had the chance to meet them all face-to-face before now. But unfortunately the world is not an ordinary place at the moment and for some of them this essay will be the first contact that I've had. Still, it will be interesting to see how they've all managed with the first topic.

However, rather than starting to work through all the new emails, I instead find myself scrolling down to an email that came in yesterday. It's an email telling me that there's a message for me on Facebook. The sender of the message is called Julie Stonor.

When I first saw this email I didn't know what to make of it. I don't know anyone called Julie Stonor.

She's not on my list of current students. What was she messaging me for? Was it spam? Was it a scam? There was a link in the email that would take me straight to the message on Facebook but I thought it was probably not a good idea to click on that. So I had opened up Facebook in my browser to take a look. And it turned out that it *was* a real message. It had been sent from a Facebook group called Tangley Wood School Class of 1986.

After studying her profile picture I was finally able to identify who Julie Stonor is. She is the Julie who was formerly known as Julie Whitworth. Her hair is different. Back in the 1980s I remember her as having a bleached, Bonnie Tyler-type hairdo but, now she's in her fifties, she seems to have moved on to a more easy-to-manage style. It's definitely her though.

I'm guessing it's probably safe now to use the link in the email, so I click it and go to the message again, It's clear that Julie has keenly embraced the social media age as her message is liberally peppered with emojis. I'm not much of a one for emojis myself. I'm not much of a one for social media at all, actually. Prior to yesterday, it had been ages since I last looked at Facebook. I read through the message again:

From: Julie Stonor.
Hi Adam. Are you the Adam Gunson who was in the Tangley Wood sixth form between 1984 and 1986? I'm thinking you might be. ☺☺ *Hoping*

you're well. I've just set up this Facebook group and we're looking at arranging a reunion for all the folks who were there back then. It will be so good for us all to get together when this lockdown thing is over and we're allowed to meet up with each other again. Would you be interested in coming along? I hope you are, it would be really great to see you there. ☺☺☺ Hey, do you remember the geography field trip? What a mad time that was! Were you one of the ones who got sent home early? Love, Julie xxx

Okay, so I'll level with you. Yes, I admit it. Since I first saw this email I've been thinking about nothing else. A Tangley Wood School reunion? I've been thinking about that constantly since I first read the message. And the geography field trip? Yes of course I remember that, Julie. I remember it like it was yesterday. I can remember it as clearly as anything.

Nestled deep in amongst all the random stuff that fills our thoughts are what you might call the big memories. The defining memories. The memories that stubbornly stick to the sides of our minds. And for me, the geography field trip is one of those memories. If you were to ask me, I'd probably tell you that my life can be divided into the time that came before the geography field trip and the time that came after.

Because in the time that came after, everything would start to be different.

Chapter 2

I guess I'm one of those people who have a good memory. People have often told me that I do. I seem to remember things that others don't. For example, I've been browsing through the posts on the Tangley Wood School Facebook group that Julie has set up. One of the items on there is a photo showing a bunch of us in the sixth form common room. Everyone is in fancy dress and some of the figures grouped in front of the camera are dressed as playing cards. Well, I say playing cards, but the costumes were really no more than bin bags with the playing card designs stuck on.

Below the photo is a whole discussion thread but no one seems to recall what had been happening. Am I the only one who remembers that the occasion was the sixth form Christmas panto, that the panto had been *Alice in Wonderland* and that the people who were dressed as playing cards had roles in the panto? I'll post a reply on there shortly and tell them the answer. And after that I really must make a start on these essays.

But yes, it does appear that I can recall details from those times that others don't seem to be able to. For instance, that first morning of the geography field trip is something that I can remember precisely. I can see it all clearly, even from this distance. If I tried, I reckon I could relive the whole thing in my imagination.

What, don't you believe me? All right then, I'll prove it to you. Come on...

It's a bright, sunny Monday morning in April 1985 and I'm walking down the main road towards the school. No school uniform for me today – we've all been allowed to wear our own clothes for the duration of the field trip. I'm looking sharp and wearing my best gear – stone-washed 620 jeans, black shirt with button-down collar, white socks and dexy grey moccasins.

I'm weighed down slightly by my sports bag which is packed for four nights away from home. My mum had offered to drive me to the school to save me walking but I had said no; I need to make a strong entrance this morning and turning up in my mum's Talbot Sunbeam isn't going to cut it. No, the bag may be heavy but I'm fine with that. I'm walking tall and the world is a brilliant place. Today is the day that my life is going to properly begin. Today I'm going on the geography field trip. And I'm going to ask Roz Madsen to go out with me.

Okay, so I probably need to give you a bit of context before I continue. A bit of backstory to the backstory, as it were. This confident decision to ask Roz Madsen out on a date had not just happened that morning. The seeds had been sown the Saturday before, when I had called round to visit Derek Hotchkiss.

Derek is my best friend. I've known him for the past eight years. We were both at primary school together. He lives in a house on the Thistledown housing estate a short BMX ride from my home. I had gone round to his on Saturday.

'You made it then?' Derek had answered the door and ushered me in with his usual acerbic welcome. I had nodded and followed him up the stairs to his room.

I've spent many afternoons over the years round at Derek's house. During that time our activities have progressed from playing with Lego and making Airfix models to playing ZX Spectrum games and listening to music. Derek has recently redecorated his bedroom – his parents allowed him to paint it partly in black, and one wall now has a newly acquired poster of Bono from U2 pinned to it. And he has a proper stereo in his room, with a turntable and a separate amplifier and all the associated gear. Derek's bedroom is considerably cooler than my own.

There had been many times in the past year where we would hang out round at Derek's and listen to music and talk about the music we had bought and the music we were going to buy. And if Derek had bought an album he thought I should know about then he would make a tape of it for me. However, in more recent weeks the music talk has been side-lined in favour of a different subject. Because for the past two months I have been in love with a girl in my A Level geography class called Roz Madsen.

When I had first confided in Derek his immediate response had been a bit surprising. Rather than laugh at me, or make a mockery of my embryonic love life, he had said, 'So what do you want to do about it?'

'How do you mean?'

'Do you want to pursue it? Or do you want to get rid of it?'

'I-I'm not sure,' I had replied, somewhat nervously. 'Pursue it, I guess.'

I had always thought this first question Derek had asked was a bit strange. Why would I want to get rid of it? This feeling that I had never known before now, this whole 'love' business, this sunshine in my stomach, it was the most incredible thing I had ever known. Why would I ever want to get rid of that?

Derek had perhaps been onto something though. Because, in all the weeks that had passed since then and now I had done precisely nothing to pursue it either. It's easy for me to make excuses for my teenage self but the truth was that, as well as my shyness and general lack of nerve, there was also a lack of opportunity; the only times I ever saw Roz was at school and, outside of geography classes, she was always with her friends. I had been unable to engineer an encounter with her where it was just the two of us.

Last Saturday's discussion with Derek had started out much the same as it had done on previous occasions:

'How's your heart?' he asked.

'It's good,' I replied.

'Still fancy Roz?'

'Yes.'

'Asked her out yet?'

'No.'

'Do you still want to?'

'Yes.'

'So are you going to?'

'Yes.'

'When are you going to then?'

'Not sure. Waiting for the right time.'

'Well it's rather chronic that you haven't asked her out yet. Isn't it?'

That day, however, the conversation took a new and potentially helpful direction. Derek was in the middle of taping me a copy of the new Phil Collins album. While doing this he asked about the upcoming field trip.

'This field trip you're going on...'

'The geography field trip?'

'Yeah. Where is it you're going?'

'Wales. Pembrokeshire.'

'Whereabouts exactly?'

'Shore Haven.'

'Which I'm guessing is somewhere near the sea?'

'Yes. It's on the coast.'

'And is Roz going too?'

'Yes.'

'Excellent. And are any of Roz's friends also going?'

'No. I don't think so.'

'What about the girls she knows in the school orchestra? Are any of them going?'

'Not as far as I know.'

'Well there you are then. You keep saying that the reason you haven't asked Roz out so far is because she's always with her friends or with other people. But if none of her friends are there then you won't have that problem. You'll be down there for, how long is it, five days? Away from the school and the gossip and all that. In a totally new place. Excellent. Adam and Roz, together by the seaside. A perfect opportunity is bound to present itself.'

'You think?'

'I'm positive. It is a well-known fact that being by the seaside can have a huge, positive effect on your chances of getting a girl to go out with you. She may still say no, of course. But she won't have any of her friends to talk to and it'll be days until you're back at school again and she'll have probably forgotten about it by then anyway.'

'You reckon?'

'Absolutely. Besides, you should be spending less time worrying about her saying no and focus more on what's gonna happen if she says yes. Make sure you've got some sort of date prepared for her. My advice would be to buy her some chips. It's the seaside so there's bound to be fish and chips nearby. Yes that's the way to go, offer to buy her some chips and then take it from there...'

And so, there I am on the first morning of the field trip, striding down the road towards the school and brimming with confidence. Talking with Derek has really helped. I feel like I can do it this time. My thoughts are filled with Roz Madsen and my heart is in a happy condition. One of the things that really struck me from our last talk was hearing Derek say the words 'Adam and Roz' in the same sentence, our two names clipped together as if he were already thinking of us as a couple. Being thought of as part of a couple; that is going to be a new thing for me. New and a bit scary, but also exciting. Yes, today is the day that I truly believe my life will properly begin.

I walk through the open gates at the front of the school. It's strange to see it so empty, no gangs of uniformed kids bundling in at the start of the day. But it's still the Easter holidays; the summer term doesn't begin until later that week. The teachers' car park is also empty. Well, I say car park. It was actually meant to be the school playground but whoever originally designed the layout had not made enough allowance for parking so it's always been used as the teachers' car park. Today though it is completely empty of cars.

On the far side of the playground is the entrance to the sports hall. This is the designated pick-up point for us field trippers and I can see some of the others are already there. I walk across to them, trying to look as cool as I can. There are a group of girls that include Julie Whitworth and Linda Sterling. As I walk over they all stop talking and look towards me and I have a sudden panic. There had been a day at school a few weeks back when, while going down the corridor between classes, I'd noticed loads of girls giving me a look and then giggling and whispering after they'd passed me. And I was thinking, hey, I must be looking good today. Maybe one of them fancies me. And so I spent the rest of the day feeling rather good about myself and then I got home and looked in the hallway mirror and saw that I'd been walking around with two massive zits on my face. I'm now suddenly thinking, has the same thing happened today? No, I reassure myself. I had scrupulously checked my appearance before leaving the house. I am confident that I am looking smooth.

There are seven of us here so far. The girls have stopped looking at me and have resumed discussing whatever girl stuff they had been talking about. I scan the faces but I'm not seeing Roz among them. This is disappointing. I've put a lot of effort in to make an impressive entrance and she isn't here to see it. I look around the others, just in case I've missed her, but there's no sign.

Two of the boys from my class, Chas Browning and Colin Winchester, are stood by the wall of the sports hall next to where the girls are. I wander over and join them, planting my sports bag between my feet. It's odd to see all of them like this, in the school grounds but not wearing school uniforms. Colin is wearing a pink Pringle jumper. Pink Pringle jumpers seem to be a fashion thing for boys at the moment.

Chas is reading the current issue of *Microcomputer World* and Colin has a motorbike magazine. I notice that they have both brought a lot more luggage than me, including multiple holdall bags, rucksacks and boot bags. Should I have packed more stuff? It's too late to worry about that now.

Parked just across from where we are standing is the familiar school minibus, a pale green Ford Transit with the words 'Tangley Wood Comprehensive School' emblazoned on the sides in large letters. I had assumed this is what we would all be travelling to Wales in. However I now see a second minibus drive in through the gates, a newer model with a plain white paint job. It parks up alongside the green one. Colin explains that the second minibus has been hired especially for the trip as there are too many of us going to fit in just one of them.

The driver's door of the white minibus opens and Mr Gardner climbs out. Mr Gardner is the teacher who will be supervising our trip. He's a geography teacher but not the one I have for my own class; the students going on this trip come from three different A Level geography classes and Mr Gardner teaches one of the other groups. I've never had Mr Gardner as a teacher so I've had no experience of what he is like. He's a tallish man with thick brown hair and a beard, the type of beard you only seem to see on geography teachers.

Another figure also appears from the passenger side of the white minibus. Mrs Lewis. Mrs Lewis is a religious studies teacher and also the school careers teacher. I wonder what she's doing here but Colin says it's for chaperone purposes; there are no women teachers in the geography department and we need to have an adult female along for the trip, apparently.

Still no sign of Roz. I know that her mum drives a beige Triumph Acclaim. I scan the school gates expectantly, hoping to see it turn in at any moment. But it doesn't appear. The next car to arrive is a metallic blue Escort XR3 with Gemma Thorneycroft driving it.

Gemma Thorneycroft was one of the first of us in our school year to take and pass the driving test. The idea of Gemma now being a qualified driver has been a painful thing to accept, especially for those boys like me who have not yet reached the age when we can start driving. However, yet more painful is the fact that Gemma's parents have bought her a car and more painful still is that the car they have bought her is an Escort XR3.

Gemma pulls up alongside the school minibus. The windows are down and the radio is playing Laser 558. Gemma's mum is in the passenger seat. Her mum has come along so she can drive the car home again rather than leave it parked at the school while we are away. Colin and Chas and I all have a similar look on our faces which basically says that it's not a cool thing to turn up driving a car that your mum then has to drive back home for you. And of course I know of far crueller voices who have expressed surprise that Gemma was able to pass the driving test at all, what with her reputation for getting drunk and all that. But in truth, we are all just insanely jealous and wish that we owned and drove an Escort XR3 ourselves.

'Makes you sick, doesn't it?' says Chas. The three of us all stare at Gemma as she opens the door and gets out. Hang on, there's someone in the back seat. Is it Roz? I hadn't considered that she might be getting a lift in with someone else instead of her mum. The passenger seat tips forward and another girl steps out. Is it Roz? No, it's Rachel Barrett. Disappointing.

With the car unloaded, Gemma's mum drives it away. Gemma and Rachel have dressed for the trip in Treasure Hunt-style jumpsuits and ankle boots. They join the other girls and are immediately as one with all the other smiles and laughing voices. That's something I've always found interesting. Stick a bunch of girls together, even girls who have never met before, and you'll find that almost immediately they'll be talking about stuff and sharing secrets as if they'd known each other all their lives. Stick a bunch of boys together and they'll just stand around silently, hands in pockets, waiting for something to happen.

A few others have also now arrived, some on foot and some by car, but there's still no sign of Roz. It's almost half past ten, which was the time we had been told we needed to be there by.

Mr Gardner steps forward. 'Right, hush up all of you,' he says. 'Let's make a start, see who's here.'

Some of the girls are continuing to quietly giggle and I think it's because of what the teachers are wearing. Both Mr Gardner and Mrs Lewis are in denim jeans. The rest of us are all mostly wearing blue jeans too. But it is a novelty to see teachers wearing denim.

Mr Gardner has a satchel-type bag from which he pulls out a register. He starts going through the list of names, marking down those present. 'Paul Armstrong? Yes. Rachel Barrett? Yes. Charles Browning...' My own name is called. 'Adam Gunson?' and I answer yes. There is still no sign of Roz by the time he gets to her place on the list. 'Rosalyn Madsen?' He looks around the group. There are a few mumblings among the group of girls but I can't hear what they are saying. Mr Gardner asks again, 'Rosalyn Madsen? Have any of you seen Rosalyn?' And then Mrs Lewis (who is somewhat shorter than Mr Gardner) pulls him aside and says something quietly in his ear. The two of them nod and exchange a few words but, infuriatingly, I can't make out what they say. Mr Gardner turns to face us again, goes back to his list and moves onto the next name: 'Robert Northwood? Yes. Stuart Seagrave? Yes. Linda Sterling...'

Everyone else is present. And then he and Mrs Lewis open up the doors at the back of the two minibuses and signal us all to start loading our bags. And we pile our luggage into the backs of the minibuses and then we all climb on board. Mr Gardner will be driving the green minibus and Mrs Lewis the white one. And we all take our seats inside and the two minibuses then start up their engines and drive out of the school gates and head on up the road in the direction of the M4 motorway. And Roz isn't there.

Chapter 3

I'm in the green minibus, on the back seat in one corner. I'm sat next to Isaac Lee. Chas and Colin are on the row in front of me and some of the girls are up front in the remaining seats alongside Mr Gardner. The two minibuses travel in convoy, heading north towards the M4 motorway, the road to Wales.

Isaac turns to me. 'Looking forward to it then, yeah?' he asks in that nasally, monotone voice of his.

'I'm sorry?'

'Shore Haven. Are you looking forward to getting there?'

'I guess so,' I mumble, trying to sound fairly non-committal. As well as sharing a geography class, Isaac and I are also in the same A Level chemistry lessons but he is not someone that I otherwise tend to hang out with. Isaac has a reputation for being a loner and is a bit weird. His full name is Isaac Edwin Lee and for a time he insisted that we all call him by that. After a while he gave up on it though, possibly because he felt it was pretentious, possibly because it sounded like the name of a serial killer, so now he's just plain Isaac Lee again. Isaac has a rather unique look – his hair is shaved at the back and sides but with a thick, lop-sided square-cut quiff on the top. I think his intention was to look like Morrissey but that hairstyle is seemingly beyond the skill of whoever cuts his hair.

'Of course,' says Isaac, 'you know what Shore Haven is famous for, don't you?'

'What's that?'

He moves his face closer to my ear in a conspiratorial sort of way. 'UFOs,'

'What?'

'U.F.O.s.' He spells it out for me one letter at a time. 'Unidentified flying objects. I've been looking into it. Turns out that Shore Haven is bang in the centre of the Welsh Triangle.'

'The Welsh Triangle?'

'Yeah. You know about the Welsh Triangle?'

I have to confess that I do not.

'It's world famous. A magnet for UFOs. There's been all manner of things going on there for the past twenty years. UFO sightings, unexplained events, paranormal stuff, second-kind encounters, third-kind encounters, you name it. Hey, d'you think we'll see something when we get there?'

'See something? What, you mean like flying saucers?'

'Yeah. Do you think we will? I do. I reckon there's gonna be all kinds of crazy stuff going down.'

I don't like to be unkind but I'm not really in the mood for a conversation with Isaac right now, particularly one about the lunatic world that he lives in. I know that *Star Wars* and *Star Trek* are popular but sci-fi is something that I'm not that much into these days. So I just mumble a vague affirmation and then reach for my sports bag which is wedged under the seat in front of me. From it I fish out Derek's Walkman and the headphones that go with it. When I had visited him on Saturday Derek had agreed to let me borrow his Walkman for the journey (I had also asked if I could borrow his black denim Levi jacket but he had said no).

I have a number of tapes in my bag, including a copy of *No Jacket Required* , the new Phil Collins album, that Derek had done for me on Saturday. I start listening to it. The first track is 'Sussudio'. This song had first come out as a single back in January and I remember that, on first hearing it, Derek had absolutely hated that song. He thought it was awful, absolutely chronic, the worst thing Phil Collins had ever done and possibly the end of his career.

I personally thought the song was okay but was a bit confused by the title. What exactly was 'Sussudio'? Of course, when we had first heard it on the radio neither of us knew how the title was written. Derek thought it was spelt with a silent 'p' at the front, like 'pseudo' or 'psycho' and was some kind of intellectual word like that (though when I pressed him about what it actually meant he was unable to answer). I, on the other hand, thought it was the name of a girl, Sue Soodio. Well, we were both wrong. It just goes to show, if you don't see a word or a name written down and don't know how it's spelt you can make a wrong assumption and end up following a completely wrong path.

Since buying the album Derek had changed his opinion of 'Sussudio' and had advised me that turning down the bass a bit made the song sound a whole lot better. I am unable to confirm this though as Derek's Walkman has no bass adjustment.

By the time I've listened to the whole album our little convoy has joined the M4 motorway and we are heading west towards Wales. In truth, though, I haven't been absorbing much of the music as, since the start of the journey, my mind has been on other things.

Where was Roz? Why wasn't she here?

The teachers were obviously aware of something, from the way they had that mini-discussion when they were taking the register. And some of the girls seem to know what's going on, too. What did they know that I didn't? The last time I had seen Roz had been in the geography lesson on the last day of the previous school term. There was nothing said then to indicate that she wouldn't be here. I knew there were some in the class who weren't coming: Mike Molins was going to miss it because he'd gone on holiday to Ibiza with his parents; and there was one kid who apparently couldn't come because his mum couldn't afford the cost. But what was going on with Roz? And then I have a thought. Maybe she's travelling by other means. Maybe she'll already be in Shore Haven when we arrive. I convince myself that all is not yet lost.

Isaac Lee has given up trying to talk to me about aliens and he is now reading *The Chronicles of Thomas Covenant.* Outside, the sun has given way to a blanket of cloud and the motorway journey is just a parade of cars and concrete bridges. I delve down into my sports bag, seeking another cassette to listen to.

At around midday we make a stop at the motorway services at Leigh Delamere. Mr Gardner is anxious about the travel time and wants this to be just a brief toilet stop. We are to have ten minutes here and no more. Everyone disembarks from our minibus and the girls immediately head off towards the shops and restaurants.

The second minibus has parked alongside us and from its side door I see Rob Northwood emerge. He is in one of the other geography classes. I had forgotten that he was going to be coming on the trip.

Rob Northwood. For much of my time at the school I had known Rob Northwood only as a name. A name that always seemed to be the centre of trouble. A name that commonly got a mention during the school assembly, the headmaster bitterly telling him to see him in his office afterwards. Rob Northwood, a name without a face, a phantom, a cypher. It was only later that I was able to match the face to the name. And of course I knew who he was. He was the guy you would see hanging around the back gate of the school with his gang, smoking and messing about and generally being a threat. He was the guy you would see prowling around during break time, menacing and bullying the smaller kids. I have been on the wrong end of him once or twice myself. He was someone you would always do your best to avoid. Today Rob Northwood is wearing DM boots (scuffed), black jeans (dirty) and a sleeveless denim jacket (also dirty). He has a bog-brush haircut, a gold earring and a face pock-marked with the scars of playground combat. One year from now corporal punishment in schools will be banned and Rob Northwood will hold the accolade of being the last ever Tangley Wood pupil to have been given the cane.

Accompanying Rob Northwood are two others from the second minibus, Paul Armstrong (one of his gang) and Martin Vickers. I'm conscious that I'm stood here on my own, an easy target for them should they choose to cause trouble. But the three of them don't come in my direction, instead they shuffle over to a nearby litter bin and hang out there.

Isaac has decided that he now wants to get something from his luggage but it's stuck underneath a pile of other bags in the back of the minibus. He starts unloading all the bags so he can get to his own. Meanwhile, Chas and Colin are getting excited about a couple of motorcycles parked nearby (a BMW R40 and some kind of Harley Davidson, apparently). Being keen to avoid Rob Northwood & Co. I wander over and join them.

Mr Gardner spots Isaac removing all the luggage and immediately pounces on him: 'Hey you, Isaac. Stop that. Stop unloading those bags. I want us on the move again soon and I don't want any delays. Leave the bags in the minibus. I repeat, all bags are to remain inside the bus.'

'But Sir,' calls out Martin Vickers, 'Gemma Thorneycroft has already gone.'

Mr Gardner does not find that funny.

Following that short stop we are all soon back in the minibuses and our passage along the M4 continues. By the time we reach the Severn Bridge it has started raining. We join a queue of vehicles at the toll gates. There is a brief bit of panic from Mr Gardner as he doesn't have the correct change in hand to pay for the toll charge. A couple of the girls sitting up front are able to help out with the correct money, which I imagine is a bit embarrassing for him.

We cross the bridge and now we are in Wales. For some reason I have been expecting Wales to look a bit different compared to England. But from the motorway it all looks much the same, aside from the road signs now being in two languages. The rain is causing the windows of the minibus to steam up so I can't see much of the outside world anyway.

I start listening to another tape – Ultravox: *The Complete Collection*. This is a tape that I bought myself, not a copy that Derek has made for me. I remember that Derek had been a bit peeved when he learnt that I had bought this tape. Apparently it was a snide thing for me to do, buying an album and then not telling him straight away that I had done so.

Another hour or so of motorway passes outside and then Mr Gardner speaks up, calling for our attention. 'Everyone, look out the windows on your left. You can see Port Talbot. As you should all remember from the work you've been doing on industrial location. Port Talbot. Biggest iron and steel works in the country. There, you can see the blast furnaces all lined up.'

Those sat on the left side of the bus wipe away the mist and we all look out the windows, across towards the indistinct shapes on the horizon. I'm fairly indifferent to it all myself and it seems like most of the others feel the same. But there is something about the Port Talbot vista that has piqued Isaac's interest.

'They don't look much like blast furnaces to me,' Isaac says. 'They don't look anything like blast furnaces. They look nothing like the diagram. You know, the blast furnace diagram.'

I do indeed know the blast furnace diagram Isaac is referring to, having had to reproduce it several times during my school career. I'm not sure what to make of Isaac's reasoning on this subject but he still persists. 'If those are real blast furnaces then why do they look nothing like the blast furnace diagram that we've been made to draw so many times? I knew there'd be some crazy stuff going down on this trip. I just knew it.'

By the time we reach our final destination the rain has reduced to a steady, nagging drizzle. Driving along the coast road into Shore Haven offers us our first view of the sea. We've been travelling for about two and a half hours since our last stop and I for one am looking forward to getting out. We are staying at the Shore Haven Hotel which is on the beachfront road, overlooking the coast. The two minibuses pull into the hotel car park and park up. The doors all open and there's a mad scramble of hands grabbing bags so everyone can get inside before the rain gets any heavier. We all troop through the front porch of the hotel and into the foyer.

With everyone assembled inside Mr Gardner addresses us. 'Right, all of you hush up and pay attention. Your rooms are all on the first floor and have already been allocated. I'll read out who's in each room. When I call your names out, one of you from each room collect your key from Mrs Lewis. You have the rest of the afternoon to get yourselves sorted out. We're meeting down here before dinner for a briefing so get yourselves down here for six o'clock.'

He starts reading through lists of names and Mrs Lewis starts handing out the room keys. Gemma Thorneycroft and Rachel Barrett are the first to be allocated their room. Gemma asks if the hotel has a lift. There is no lift, she will have to manage with the stairs. While waiting I glance around at my new surroundings. It's a spectacularly drab-looking place. I recall that Gemma had been hoping that the hotel would have a sun room to allow her to do some work on her tan. I think she's going to be disappointed.

I hear my name called and the news is not good. I am sharing a room with Martin Vickers and Stuart Seagrave. I used to be at primary school with Martin Vickers. We sat at the same table for a time but he was always a long way from being my friend and currently he appears to be hanging out with Rob Northwood. And Stuart Seagrave, yeah, he's well known as being the most unpopular kid in the whole school.

Seagrave immediately starts protesting. 'Mr Gardner, that can't be right. There must be some mistake.'

'No mistake, Stuart. You're sharing Room Twelve with Martin and Adam.'

'But I asked for a single room.'

'No single rooms. You all have to share.'

'But I specifically – '

Mr Gardner ignores him and continues calling out names.

Meanwhile, Martin Vickers (who appears to now get all his clothing from the army surplus store) has collected the key from Mrs Lewis. He bounds speedily up the stairs, his boots rattling the wooden floorboards as he goes. I trudge after him. The stairs lead to a gloomy, narrow corridor with a long line of doors either side. Our room, Room Twelve, is about halfway down.

The condition of the room matches the rest of the hotel. There is a double bed down the centre and a couple of bunk beds against one wall. There is a TV and a desk and a door with, I'm guessing, a bathroom beyond. The wallpaper was presumably once a crisp shade of white but that was years ago and it has now faded to the colour of sun-bleached bone. Martin and I stand there for a moment, silently ingesting the ambience of the place.

And then Stuart Seagrave comes in, dragging a massive suitcase behind him. 'This is so unfair,' he starts whining. 'I was specifically promised I would have a room of my own.'

'What's the matter Seagrave?' says Martin. 'You not want to share with us? Are we not good enough for you? I'm not exactly over the moon about having to share with you either.'

Seagrave turns away, surveying the room. He sees the double bed in the centre and the bunk beds at the side and, quick as a flash, he makes his move. 'Right, I'm having the bed then.'

'You are not' says Martin. 'That bed is mine.'

'No. I have to have the bed.'

'I'm having the bed. I was here first. You can have the bunk.'

'I can't sleep in the bunk. Look at it. It's only big enough for a child.'

'Well you'll just have to make do, won't you? I'm having the bed.'

'I have to have the bed. Because of my asthma.'

Martin shakes off his flak jacket, revealing an AC/DC tee shirt underneath. He dumps his jacket on the double bed, proclaiming it as his territory. Seagrave picks up the jacket and moves it to the lower bunk bed. Martin puts it back on the double bed. This sequence continues for some time.

I walk over to the window and pull back the net curtains to look out. On any normal day this window would probably have been showing me an extremely fine view of the sea. But it's still raining outside and the windows have fogged over and there is nothing much to see except my own reflection. Right up to our arrival I have been harbouring that faint hope that Roz would be there already, waiting for us, waiting for me. But she isn't there and I now know for sure that she never will be. There I am, miles from home, in a shabby hotel on a miserable day. Roz isn't there and Derek isn't there and I am sharing a room with Martin Vickers and Stuart Seagrave.

Welcome to my own, personal hell.

Chapter 4

As I mentioned, Martin Vickers is someone I am a bit wary of. My reasons for this date back to our time at primary school. Specifically, I can pin it down to an incident at age eight on the school playing field. While running around with all the other kids playing some game or other, I tripped and fell to the ground and ended up bawling my eyes out in pain with a large twig sticking out of my left leg. The consensus of the school nurse and all the other adults was that it was an accident, an unfortunate thing that could have happened to any child at any time. I, though, have always had doubts about it having been an accident. The reason for this is my memory of looking up while writhing in agony and, through my tears, seeing Martin Vickers staring down at me and uttering the words, 'Ha ha, you have fallen into my trap!'

So yes, I'm a bit wary of Martin.

After five minutes of back-and-forth arguing over who gets the double bed, Stuart Seagrave has stormed out, proclaiming that the situation is totally unacceptable and he is going to demand that Mr Gardner assign him to a different room. And I am left alone with Martin. We share a glance, acknowledging each other from opposite sides of the double bed. Does he remember our playing field encounter from all those years ago? If he has forgotten I can easily remind him. I literally have the scars to show for it. But instead he turns and mutters, 'Huh, that's just brilliant, that is.'

'What's that?' I ask.

'Having to share a room with a bloody nark.'

'Oh.' I nod back at him. 'Yeah, right.'

Of course I know what he's referring to. He's referring to the reason why Stuart Seagrave is the most unpopular kid in the school. He is referring to the catastrophe that was the sixth form party.

The sixth form party had been staged at Manfreds nightclub in Woking the previous autumn. Some of the upper sixth formers had organised it and were openly selling tickets in the common room during the weeks beforehand. I remember at the time that we were all really excited at the prospect of this party and I was certainly looking forward to it. But what the upper sixth formers had failed to allow for was that Manfreds was an adults-only nightclub. Under eighteens were not allowed in, and us lower sixth formers were all still under age. Many of us had voiced our concerns about the difficulties we might encounter trying to get into the place, despite having bought tickets, and these fears did prove to be correct.

I remember that night well – a whole bunch of us boys stood around in the shopping centre outside the club doors. We watched the likes of Linda Sterling and Rachel Barrett, with their ra-ra skirts and glitter make-up and permed hairdos, walk straight through the door, no questions asked, but us sixteen-year-old boys were all being turned away by the bouncers, betrayed by our spotty faces and lack of visible maturity.

As well as the age policy the club also had a dress code – no jeans, no trainers, you had to be wearing formal shoes and a respectable jacket with collar and tie. In the adjacent shop doorways there were crazy scenes of clothes-swapping deals going on. Some boys had come well-dressed but were being turned away because they looked too young. Others had turned up in the wrong clothes and were doing trades with the unsuccessful kids, borrowing shoes, jackets, sometimes even trousers, to see if they had any better luck getting inside.

I was with Derek and a few other boys and we did manage to get in at the third attempt without showing ID (which was just as well since we had none) following a change of personnel on the door. The whole time I spent in that place was fairly uncomfortable as I feared I might be apprehended and thrown out at any moment. However there were plenty of boys who had not been able to get in at all, even though they had tickets. And of those, one had complained to his parents and his parents had complained to the school and the school had complained to the club and the police had got involved and the club had been fined for allowing underage drinking. The fallout of it all was that the headmaster had banned all future sixth form parties.

It was widely believed that the boy who had complained was Stuart Seagrave. And he had been hated for it ever since.

So yes, when Martin says he is unhappy about sharing a room with Stuart Seagrave I know where he's coming from. I don't really want to hang around with Martin either though, so I make my excuses and head off to explore the rest of the hotel and its surrounding area.

About twenty minutes later I am standing outside, in front of the sea wall, looking out across Shore Haven beach. The rain has stopped and it looks like it might turn out to be a nice evening.

The Shore Haven Hotel faces out onto the coast road with the sea wall and beach directly in front. The beach is wide, about one mile across with rocky cliffs enclosing it at each end; the knowledge I have gleaned from years of geography classes tell me that the place I am looking at would correctly be described as a cove. Or a bay. Or possibly an inlet. I note that Julie Whitworth and Linda Sterling have also ventured out to take a look around. They take a brief look at the sea and then head off up the road towards where some shops are visible.

Directly in front of the hotel, on the other side of the road and behind the sea wall, is a small, single-story building. It has a sign on it that reads 'Cocktail Club.' It looks like it was once part of the hotel as it had been painted in the same colour scheme of white stone and dark blue woodwork. But that must have been years ago as the place is now obviously abandoned and derelict. The paint is virtually all gone from the timbers, there are large chunks of masonry missing and the letters on the sign are so faded that they are only just visible. It looks as if it might collapse at any moment.

To the left of the Cocktail Club is an iron bench, worn and corroded from decades of coastal weathering. It's still wet from the earlier rain so, rather than sit on it, I stand behind it, leaning against the back, and gaze out across the beach towards the horizon. It's low tide at the moment and the sand extends out a long way. The beach faces west so, if the sky clears up, it should provide for a really splendid-looking sunset later. I should be stood here with Roz right now, looking at this view with her, just like Derek had said.

What was it about Roz that had made me fall in love with her? Derek had asked me that several times and I had never really been able to give a good answer. Was it down to some specific feature of hers? Like her having the most delicate, shell-like ears, or a face that was a perfect oval? Or was it because her hair blazed like a

Monet sunrise, or because her eyes sparkled like a lime cocktail on a poolside bar in a Wham! video? I honestly don't know. I'm not even sure I would actually choose to describe her in these kinds of ways. Don't get me wrong. I mean, she did have red hair and green eyes and a face and she did look really nice. But I don't think there was any one thing, I think it was just all of her; she seemed to me to be totally everything. All I know for sure is that I had woken up one morning two months ago and had found that I was suddenly in love with Roz Madsen. I don't know how or why or where it came from, I only know that it is something that happened to me. I suppose you might call it a passion.

Stuart Seagrave has emerged from the hotel entrance. He walks straight past me – either he's ignoring me or he hasn't seen me. He continues down the steps in the sea wall and out onto the beach. I had considered venturing down onto the beach myself but it doesn't look that inviting. There's sand and shingle but also areas of what look like black mud or tar. The beach also appears to have a liberal sprinkling of litter and dead things on it. Seagrave carries on, striding out towards the edge of the tide.

What more can I tell you about Stuart Seagrave? He is a total misfit. The school had plenty of kids like Isaac who were a bit strange, a bit oddball, but they did at least seem to belong there. Seagrave, though, is in a whole other league, a complete outsider. He is tall and gangly, a collection of stick-thin arms and legs and he has a head shaped like a peanut. He has acquired various playground nicknames over the years, such as 'Inspector Gadget,' 'Pipecleaner Boy' and 'The Small Intestine.' Whenever I had heard him speak up in class (which was often) he had this thin, whiney voice that cut straight through you like a cheese wire.

He is such a swot and is always sucking up to the teachers. For example, I remember this one time during a French lesson. The teacher was talking about how 'monsieur' literally means 'my sir' and 'madame' means 'my lady.' And Seagrave pipes up and says, 'Oh, so I suppose that "mademoiselle" literally means "my damsel" then?' I mean, come on. You can't go saying things like that in a French class at a modern comprehensive school and think the kids are going to respect you for it.

There was a rumour that Seagrave had originally been at some smart, private boarding school and he had only ended up at Tangley Wood Comprehensive because his parents couldn't afford the fees. He never seemed to hang out with anyone or have any friends.

I watch as he continues walking out towards the edge of the tide. Is he wearing flared trousers? Jesus, he is as well. I can see the bottoms of them flapping around in the breeze. How could a kid be so square? I mean, it's like he's from another world or something. No wonder he's always being picked on and ridiculed; if you wear trousers like that in 1985 you're just asking for trouble.

They are strange things, trousers. I remember a time not so long ago when a pair of trousers was just a pair of trousers, no more than that. As a kid of nine or ten your mum would buy you new trousers and you just wore what you were given. I must have had flared trousers back then because I remember how they used to always be getting caught in my bike chain. But I didn't think anything of it, that just seemed to be the way trousers were.

But then suddenly, at about the age of thirteen I must have become a whole lot more self-aware. Because, all at once, flared trousers just simply would not do. They had to be straight and narrow. I remember begging my mum to get me some new school uniform trousers with straight legs. Yes, at age thirteen I definitely started noticing things like trousers. And girls.

I decide to take a wander up the road to where the shops and other buildings are. There's an adjoining road with some more shops including a newsagents and a post office and a seedy-looking pub called the Admiral Totty. Despite being next to the sea, Shore Haven does not appear to have a whole lot of business aimed at the tourist trade. There is a fish and chip shop though, on the far corner of the street. I recall what Derek had said – I should be in that fish and chip shop right now with Roz, buying her some chips. But that's not happening and instead there I am wandering the pavements like a loser.

I catch sight of Julie and Linda up ahead, stood outside the post office and sharing a newly-opened bag of Opal Fruits. They obviously know something about the reason Roz isn't here. What I should be doing is going up to them and asking them the question. But if I do that they are bound to ask me why I'm interested in Roz and I'll have to either tell them the truth or make up some lie which is certain to sound unconvincing. I decide not to.

Having taken in the general look and feel of the place, I turn to head back to the hotel, only to find myself suddenly face to face with Isaac. His creeping up on me like that startles me.

'Psst, seen anything yet?' he asks. 'Any alien activity?'

I tell him I have not.

'No, me neither. There's definitely something about this place though. Something in the air. Something not right. As if there's layers of crazy stuff hidden just below the surface. Hey, you know how it is in O Level chemistry when you learn about atoms and how atoms have electrons orbiting round them like planets orbiting the sun. And that all seems nice and simple and straightforward.

'And then you start doing A Level chemistry and it turns out the stuff they told you in O Level chemistry wasn't true at all. The orbits the electrons are in are not simple orbits like planets, there are orbits within orbits. And they're not orbits at all, they are shells, and the electrons are not like particles, they are more like a smear, part particle and part wave. They start off telling you that atoms are simple things but it turns out there's all these extra, hidden layers of complexity.

'And everything's connected. You think that the universe is just made up of random bits of stuff, but no, everything is connected to everything else in all kinds of secret ways.

'This place is like that. Don't you reckon? Look around you. It all appears ordinary on the surface but underneath there are hidden layers of complexity. Hidden connections. Things we don't know about. Orbits within orbits. Wheels within wheels. There's something coming soon, I can sense it.'

'Seriously?' I ask. 'Are you seriously expecting to see a flying saucer?'

'All I'm saying is,' Isaac says, his voice dropping to a furtive whisper, 'don't be surprised if, at some stage while you're here, you have a life changing encounter that involves creatures from another world.'

'You really think that?'

'Yeah. And don't go talking to anyone else about this. There's no telling who you can trust around here. The person you think is your friend may really be an alien duplicate from a pod. So say nothing. Keep it dark, okay?'

I make my excuses, with a promise to Isaac that I will keep watching the skies, and head back down the road. Returning to the hotel, I notice that there is now another minibus in the car park, a yellow one with the words 'Kimble College' on its side. I guess it should be no surprise that another bunch of students would be here at the same time as us. Isaac may say that Shore Haven is famous for UFO sightings but to me it's looking more like the capital city of geography field trips.

I glance out across the beach but I can't see Seagrave out there. There's no sign of him. Where is he, I wonder. Maybe he's gone. Maybe his indignation at having to share a room is so great that he's left and gone away. Or maybe a flying saucer has indeed landed on the beach, unseen, and taken him back to his home planet.

I return to the hotel. Seagrave, it turns out, has not disappeared and is back up in the room. It seems that he and Martin have somehow reached a settlement regarding the double bed.

'You know what, Seagrave? Bollocks to it.' Martin is now sat on the lower bunk bed reading a *Commando* comic. 'I don't care anymore. You can have the bed. And you know why? Because I'm prepared to be the bigger man here, that's why.'

'Thank you,' says Seagrave. 'That's very mature of you.'

'By the way, Gardner came by while you two were out. He gave me the instructions for the field work we'll be doing while we're here. The three of us are all in the same working group.'

'What, you mean I'm going to be stuck working with you all day as well as sharing this room?'

'Hey, I don't like it either, but we're just gonna have to make do.'

'Oh, that's great, that is. Just great.'

I retrieve my sports bag from where I had left it, in the corner by the radiator. In doing so I notice there's now a patch of black mud that has been trodden into the carpet. The carpet wasn't exactly in showroom condition before but now it looks absolutely disgusting. It appears to be the same type of black mud that I noticed was on the beach. Seagrave must have done it. He must have got the mud on his shoes while he was out there and brought it in with him. Neither Seagrave nor Martin appear to have noticed it. I'm wondering whether I really should say something about the mud.

Seagrave, oblivious to the mess he has made, has started on his own unpacking. His luggage is comprised of a large, well-travelled old suitcase. He huffily hauls it up and opens it so it now covers half the bed. Martin and I watch as Seagrave proceeds to unpack, filling up all the drawer space with his stuff. It seems as if he has brought everything that he owns.

'Bloody hell, Seagrave!' Martin just can't help himself sticking a bit more needle in. 'How much crap have you brought with you? We're only here for five sodding days.'

'It does no harm to be prepared,' Seagrave snips back at him. 'Just because you haven't brought any change of clothes with you. Not all of us choose to live like vagrants.'

It is true that Martin has travelled light; the only stuff he has brought with him are the contents of a Virgin Megastore carrier bag.

'Oh come on.' Martin is leafing through the items that are now scattered across the bed. 'What's this you've brought? Epsom salts? Diarrhoea tablets? Ex-Lax chocolate?'

'Just taking precautions. Unfamiliar food often has a bad effect on my bowels.'

'Are you sure you need all this? Talcum powder, moisturiser, foot powder, sun cream, zit cream, Mandate aftershave. Hey, you do realise that if you're trying to get off with a girl then this stuff isn't going to do it for you?'

'Shut up, Vickers.' Seagrave appears offended by the very suggestion. 'Some of us just happen to not like being dirty. Some of us prefer to wash ourselves properly in the morning.'

'What are you saying, Seagrave? Are you saying I'm dirty?'

'All I am saying is that there is nothing wrong with a person wanting to keep themselves clean. Not everyone has the hygiene habits of Captain Caveman.'

'Yeah, well some of us are able to keep ourselves clean without having to rely on rubbish like this. All a man needs is a basic bar of soap and some hot water. Look at Gunson there. Does he look like a bloke who spends ages pampering his face every day? Of course he doesn't.'

While speaking, Martin has been inspecting Seagrave's electric razor. The razor is a high quality one but looks to be about ten years old. Maybe it's something his dad has passed onto him. 'Hey, leave that alone.' Seagrave snatches the razor back off him. 'And don't think I'm letting you borrow my sun cream either.'

'I don't want your sun cream. Real men don't use sun cream. Real men don't use any of the crap you've brought with you. Hey, what's this? Looks like a Japanese wanking ring.'

'What? No of course it isn't. Will you please just leave my stuff alone.' Seagrave is sounding like he's close to losing it.

'Hey, there'd better not be any funny stuff in the night. I don't want to be listening to you tossing yourself off under the bedspread.'

'Shut up Vickers.'

'I'm serious Seagrave. This isn't your old public school dormitory. If you're going to be spending your time spunking up then you can find some other place to do it. Some place where I'm not around.'

'SHUT UP WILL YOU! JUST SHUT UP!'

I take myself off to the bathroom and reflect on my current situation. Is this what it's going to be like, sharing a room for the next five days with these two at each other's throats? I wish Derek was here. I wish I was sharing a room with him instead. Why did he decide not to pick geography as one of his A Levels?

One of the subjects Derek is doing is Latin. What is he doing Latin for? Learning how to converse in a dead language and translating chunks of *Caesar's Gallic Wars* – what's the good of that? Geography is a much better subject to be studying. It's all nice and straightforward. There's no need for you to question anything or think for yourself or have your own opinion about anything. Geography lessons mostly involve copying down what the teacher has written on the blackboard. Geography is my kind of subject. Why couldn't Derek have chosen geography instead of Latin? I curse him for his academic choices.

Chapter 5

I really need to make a start on marking these essays. Time is ticking by and I can't waste the whole day dwelling on the past and trying to relive events that happened decades ago.

The subject of the first essay of the year is concerned with Isaiah Berlin's 'Two Concepts of Liberty.' Positive and negative freedom. This is one of my favourite topics and I'm always interested to see what a new set of students have to say about it.

Maybe if the first essay I read through is of a decent standard then that might give me some encouragement. Let's open it up and give it a try. This first essay is from a student called Rupert.

My attempts at finding motivation prove to be short-lived, though. Because, sad to say, Rupert's essay does not seem to display a good grasp of what Berlin was going on about. He has gone down the familiar line of describing negative freedom as being 'freedom from' restrictions and positive freedom as 'freedom to' do things. I know the set text book frames it in those terms but I've never really cared for that way of describing it myself.

I've always thought that a better approach is to think of positive and negative freedom in terms of internal and external barriers. To put it simply, having negative freedom means not being inhibited by external constraints. For example, if someone has tied me up and locked me in a box then you would say I am lacking in negative freedom. Positive freedom, on the other hand, is about having the ability to achieve certain desired life goals. To elaborate, I might want to gain an academic qualification in order to get a better job and provide a better life for my family. But if, rather than doing all the work that this involves I instead choose to go out drinking and gambling then you would say I am lacking in positive freedom. Positive freedom is having the ability to be the kind of person you want to be.

Another way of looking at it, that someone told me once, is to think of it in terms of doors. Negative freedom is about doors being open to you, rather than locked, and positive freedom is about being able to walk through those doors.

The second part of the essay relates to how theories based on positive freedom have been misused by various political ideologies throughout history. Berlin has a fair bit to say about this. And this is where positive freedom gets something of a bad reputation. You've had various totalitarian regimes in the past enacting policies based on the ideas of Karl Marx and Jean-Jacques Rousseau. They have claimed that their citizens should be forced to live their lives in a certain, specific way on the grounds that it's ultimately what's best for everyone. But, like Berlin says, people are not all the same. We all have different desires and goals and views about how we want to live our lives. And any attempt by a dictatorship to impose a single way of living onto everyone is always going to end badly. Because that's the thing about positive freedom. You might well demonstrate it by choosing and living the life that you want to live, by being the person that you want to be, but the only person who can make that choice is you. Someone else's idea of positive freedom should never be forced onto you. Not by other people, not by governments.

This part of the essay represents forty percent of the total mark. However Rupert seems to have rather skimped over this bit and doesn't say much about it at all. Not the best of starts. But then again, this is the first piece of work I've had from him. He just needs a bit of guidance, a bit of feedback on what is expected. I must not be too judgemental of a student's initial efforts.

I should really be pushing on and getting the rest of these essays marked. But I just can't concentrate. My mind keeps dragging itself back to other things. Back to that week in 1985...

It is ten o'clock on the first full day of the field trip. Martin Vickers, Stuart Seagrave and I are standing on a

Pembrokeshire beach. Not the Shore Haven beach in front of the hotel, no, another beach further up the coast. It is a massive, wide beach in front of a high cliff face. It's a fine morning beneath a clear, blue sky. We are embarked on the first of our field study tasks: to examine how the process of longshore drift has brought about the arrangement of pebbles on the beach. We are to inspect and record the pebbles at the foot of the cliff, their size, shape, material and general distribution.

Following breakfast Mr Gardner had given us a full briefing on how we should do this. At the end of the morning we are to have a usable set of data concerning the pebbles. Once back at the hotel we are to analyse our data and write it up as a piece of project work. And this written work should form a neat presentation on the topic of longshore drift with conclusions as to why the pebbles are organised on the beach the way they are. That is the reason we are there. Pebbles.

To be honest with you, pebbles or no pebbles, I am not feeling at my absolute perkiest this morning. This is because I got very little sleep during the night. There are three causes for this.

The first cause of my not sleeping well was the cold: Room Twelve is a very cold room. This was perhaps to be expected, what with it being on the side of the hotel that is most exposed to the elements. The coldness would probably have been less of an issue had I been wearing pyjamas, but I had chosen not to. Because, when Seagrave had emerged from the bathroom wearing his own set of floral-patterned jimjams, Martin had immediately started ridiculing him. 'Seagrave, you are such a gimp. A proper man doesn't wear pyjamas like those. A proper man doesn't wear pyjamas at all, he sleeps in his pants.'

I too had brought pyjamas with me but I now made an immediate decision not to wear them. Yes I admit it, I was bowing to peer pressure. I followed Martin's lead and bedded down for the night wearing just my boxer shorts. I had never slept in just my pants before and I did not have a comfortable time of it. Plus I hadn't realised how cold the night was going to be. The room had radiators but there was no heat coming out of them. So there I was, in the lower of the two bunk beds with the bulk of Martin Vickers hanging over me, shivering underneath a bri-nylon sheet and an orange blanket.

The second cause of my not sleeping well was Roz: I had of course spent many nights before now being unable to sleep due to thoughts of Roz dancing around in my head. But this time was even worse; all my hopes and plans of resolving the situation had received a serious set-back.

And the third cause? That was Seagrave. For the whole night Seagrave had been lying in that double bed, comfortably asleep but at the same time making the most unbelievable amount of noise. Was it snoring? Was it sleep apnoea? God only knows. But whatever it was, he was wheezing and belching right through until dawn and it was impossible to get any sleep.

Martin had plainly had a disturbed night as well. 'What the hell's the matter with you?' he complained the next morning. 'Jesus, how are the rest of us supposed to sleep with you making all that noise?'

'It's not my fault,' Seagrave had protested. 'It's my asthma. There must be some dust in the room that set me off.'

'You make more noise when you're asleep than you do when you're awake.'

And, sadly, there was worse to come. Seagrave's problems, we soon established, were not confined to just his night time breathing; he also had an issue with his guts which developed into a severe bout of farting.

'Bloody hell! What is it with you? Are you trying to stink the place out so you have the room all to yourself? Is that your plan?'

'I'm sorry but it's not my fault. I told you I had problems with my guts. It's that pork they gave us for dinner last night. Obviously the meat hadn't been cooked properly.'

'You are unbelievable, Seagrave. You've got gas blowing out of you at both ends. One end by day and the other by night.'

'I said I'm sorry. Will you please not keep going on about it.'

'I can't be doing with this anymore. I'm going to ask Gardner to be moved to a different room.'

'Fine. I'm going to ask the same thing. I can't stand another night with you either.'

So the three of us went downstairs and during breakfast they both pleaded with Mr Gardner to be moved to a different room, both insisting that they could not spend another night in the same place as the other. It was still to no avail though, Mr Gardner had told them both to hush up and to get on with things the way they were.

In fact Mr Gardner was not having a good start to the day as there were complaints coming in from other directions as well. Gemma Thorneycroft and Linda Sterling were both moaning about their rooms being too cold and the showers not working properly. I personally had resolved that I was just going to keep my head down and not get involved with any of it. I just wanted to get through the next four days. Honestly, for me the end of the week couldn't come soon enough.

While we were having our breakfast I noticed the kids from the other school that were also staying at the hotel. They were at the other end of the restaurant, sat round a long table like we were. There were nine of them in total, boys and girls about the same age as us. Some of them were wearing yellow jumpers with the words 'Kimble College' across the front; others had less formal tee-shirts proclaiming that 'Kimbleens Rule OK!' I caught sight of them again later, in the carpark, gathered round their own minibus as ours were driving away. I wondered whether they were going to the same place as us. But no, their destination was apparently elsewhere.

So there we are, picking pebbles up off the beach and noting down their size, shape and location. Well I say we, but so far it's just been me and Seagrave doing it. Martin, instead of working, is stood staring towards a point fifty yards away where Julie Whitworth and Linda Sterling are doing their own pebble study. The air is warmer this morning and Linda has dressed for the beach, in a skimpy red tee-shirt and white pedal pushers.

'Vickers. Are you going to help us with this,' complains Seagrave, 'or are you going to spend all morning staring at the girls?'

'That Linda's got nice tits.' Martin observes.

'What?'

'Linda. I've never noticed before. She's got nice tits.'

'You can't say that.'

'Why not? It's a compliment isn't it? Hey, Gunson. Do you think Linda's got nice tits? Of course he does. See?'

'You can't talk about her like that.'

'Why not? She can't hear us.'

'It's disrespectful.'

'Disrespectful? What, do you fancy her then? Do you want to go out with her? You do, don't you!'

'No I don't. Absolutely not.'

'So why am I being disrespectful then?'

'Because you just are. Why? Do *you* want to go out with her?'

'No.'

'But you just said she's got nice tits.'

'Yeah, but you don't go out with a girl just because she's got nice tits.'

'Oh, right. So, do please tell us, what does make you want to go out with a girl then?'

'You go out with a girl,' says Martin, after a moment's contemplation, 'if she's got nice tits, and a nice face, and a nice hairdo.'

'Really? So you're now saying that Linda doesn't have a nice face?'

'No. No, I'm not saying she's a digby.'

'A digby?'

'Yeah. You know, the biggest dog in the world. I'm not saying she's that. No, no, I just wouldn't go out with her because she goes to our school. I wouldn't go out with any girl who goes to Tangley Wood School on a matter of principle.'

'A matter of principle?' Seagrave lets drop the pebble he has just been measuring. 'Well I'm sure,' he concludes, 'that all the girls in the sixth form will be very pleased to hear that you feel that way. Now come on, will you please stop messing around and help get this work done.'

'Hey, there's no need to get all stroppy,' says Martin. 'We've got plenty of time to do this crap. We've got all morning.'

'Mr Gardner told us to be finished and back at the minibuses by eleven.'

'Exactly. Plenty of time.' Martin has now steered his attention to the cliff face behind us. 'Hey, I wonder if I could climb that? I wonder if I could climb up there to the top.'

'What? No. Don't be stupid.'

'An SAS commando could climb up there, no problem.'

'Yes, but you're not an SAS commando.'

'I could be.'

'Just because you wear the same jacket as the SAS does not automatically mean you have the same skills. Honestly Vickers, you're such a juvenile.'

Martin shakes his head. 'I reckon I can do it.' He walks off, picking his way over the rock pools towards the base of the cliff and Seagrave, after further protest, throws his hands up in despair.

I have chosen to keep myself right out of all this and have been quietly measuring and recording the stones. I continue for another five minutes or so and then I pick up a pebble that seems unlike the others. It feels somehow different. Made of a different material. I turn it over in my fingers. There appears to be some writing on the other side, obscured by some sand and dirt. I rub away the dirt so I can read it more clearly. Some letters have been inked onto it with a thick, black felt pen. 'Hey, look at this.' I call Seagrave over. 'This one's got something written on it.'

'What?'

'There's writing on it. See?'

'What does it say?'

'Take a look'

I hand the pebble to Seagrave. He reads it. '"Principal Parts".'

Martin, meanwhile, has given up on his attempt to climb the cliff. The SAS commando has returned, his mission incomplete. 'What're you doing now?'

'Adam found a pebble with writing on it.'

'What? Giss it here.' Martin snatches the pebble and inspects it. '"Principal Parts".' You can see his mind working while his eyes are looking it over. 'What does it mean?'

'No idea.'

'Principal parts? Principal parts of what?'

None of us have any idea what it means. Seagrave and I can offer nothing but blank faces in response.

'Why would anyone want to write that on a stone?' Martin ponders it for a couple of moments and then plainly loses interest in the puzzle. It looks like he's shaping up to throw the pebble into the sea, but instead he tosses it back to me.

I turn back to Seagrave. 'Should we record this one on the log then?'

'No, ignore it. Looks like it's been put here deliberately. It's not a natural part of the beach.'

I consider just chucking it away myself but instead I slip it into the pocket of my anorak and then continue, picking up the next pebble from beside my feet.

We finish looking at pebbles at about a quarter to eleven. Seagrave isn't convinced we have enough data but time has run out and we need to get back to the meeting point. The minibuses are parked up at the top of the cliff; to get to them we need to climb a set of stone steps cut into the rock, the same ones we had come down earlier to get to the beach.

The sun is starting to get strong now. Seagrave, cautious character that he is, pulls a wide-brimmed blue hat from his rucksack and puts it on. I'm expecting Martin to wind up Seagrave some more over this latest fashion choice but, to my surprise, Martin says nothing.

There is only one set of cliff steps up to the top and all the others who were working on the beach have been heading to the same point. Julie and Linda have got there before us and are already heading up. Rob Northwood and Paul Armstrong reach the base of the steps at the same time as us three. Martin exchanges a few words with them – from what I can gather those two have done only limited geography work this morning and instead had found a place among the rocks to have a smoke.

The cliff steps make for quite a steep climb but we make it up to the top okay. Some of the others have already arrived and are stood next to where the minibuses are parked.

One thing that I had noticed earlier, and notice again now, is that many of our party are wearing solid, serious-looking walking boots. I am wearing my Dunlop Green Flash trainers. Dunlop Green Flash are my favourites. They may not be as professional as some of the other footwear on show today, but they look good. I'm confident they will see me right.

We are joined by Mr Gardner and Mrs Lewis. Mr Gardner starts to do a debrief on the morning's activity but then Mrs Lewis notices a couple of our group are missing.

'Charles and Colin, where are they?'

We all look around. There is no sign of Chas Browning or Colin Winchester.

'I can see them,' shouts out Gemma Thorneycroft. 'There. Down on the beach.'

We all look over the cliff. Two figures are visible, heading along the beach in a northerly direction, away from us.

'What are they doing?' Mr Gardner asks. 'Why the hell are they going in that direction?'

Mr Gardner and some of the others call out to them, arms waving, trying to get their attention, but to no avail. We all shout as loud as we can but there's no response, they haven't heard us. After yet more shouting and waving, a cursing and panic-ridden Mr Gardner scrambles down the cliff steps after them. He is not a happy man.

Mr Gardner is not my usual geography teacher so I don't know him well, but from what I've seen of him so far he does appear to be a bit highly strung. I'm guessing he doesn't have much toleration for messing about. The previous evening we had all met up in the hotel lounge prior to getting our dinner. Mr Gardner had taken this opportunity not only to brief us on the activities we would be doing while there but also to lay down what was expected of us. We were not on holiday, we were there to work. While we were there we were ambassadors for Tangley Wood Comprehensive School and that was a role that we were to take seriously. There was to be no tomfoolery of any kind. No bad behaviour, no drinking or smoking, no parties in rooms and most definitely no improper liaisons with anyone of the opposite sex. We were expected to complete the writing up of the day's fieldwork each evening after dinner and we were to all be in our rooms by nine o'clock. The hotel bar was off limits at all times and no one was to leave the hotel during the evenings. If any of us were caught transgressing any of these rules then there would be serious consequences; potentially you would be forced to pack your bags, be driven to the nearest train station and put on the next train home.

As I say, I haven't had much experience of Mr Gardner as a teacher before, but the murmurings I have heard from those in his geography class are that he is not a man you want to get on the wrong side of. Colin Winchester had told me that you can tell when Mr Gardner is in an anxious mood because his beard starts to bristle; I think I had already glimpsed signs of that this morning.

About half an hour has passed before Mr Gardner staggers back up the cliff steps, followed by a contrite-looking Chas and Colin. At the start of the day each group had been given an OS map (Seagrave had taken charge of ours) along with the coordinate locations of where we would be working. Our second activity of the day is to be on the top of the cliff, just north of where we are currently. Chas and Colin had mistakenly thought they could walk to it along the beach. They were wrong, though, and Mr Gardner is not happy about the wasted time.

We all get into the minibuses for the short journey to the next site, but thanks to the efforts of Chas and Colin there is now a bit of a grey mood hanging over us; Mr Gardner has planned the day's itinerary very closely and is not pleased about delays.

Inside the minibus I am once again sat alongside Isaac Lee. I seem to have become a magnet for that guy.

'Hey,' he starts up again, 'I've been thinking about those blast furnaces. The ones we saw yesterday. There's definitely something not right there. They look nothing like the diagram. This definitely needs more investigation.'

I nod sagely while he talks, staring out the window as we drive along a narrow, leafy lane. Isaac needs to stop dwelling on things like he does. It's not healthy.

Our second task of the day concerns the study of glacial deposits – bits of shale and slate that were deposited by a glacier during the last ice age. The technical name for this, according to our worksheets, is till fabric analysis. By recording the orientation of these pieces of rock you can work out which direction the glacier was moving in, apparently.

Mr Gardner starts briefing us on the work we have to do. He also draws our attention to the sea stacks that are just visible on the edge of the cliffs at the far end of the bay. These sea stacks, he reminds us, are the result of millions of years of coastal erosion. Whilst perhaps not as impressive as the examples we have studied in the classroom (e.g. The Needles, Isle of Wight), they are still noteworthy none the less. However Mr Gardner's commentary is suddenly and rudely interrupted by the very loud sound of someone farting.

'Right, who did that?' Mr Gardner barks at us. 'Who was it?'

I immediately know that the culprit is Seagrave as I recognise the sound from earlier. Everyone starts laughing. Even Mrs Lewis has a tiny smile showing on her lips. But Mr Gardner is absolutely fuming.

'Seagrave!' shouts Martin, 'For Christ's sake not again!'

The whole group starts giggling.

'Come on, who did that?' It's true what they say about Mr Gardner. When he gets angry you really can see his beard start to bristle.

More giggling.

'Come on, who was it?'

'It's Seagrave, Sir,' says Martin. 'Like I was telling you earlier. Me and Gunson have been having to put up with that all morning,'

Mr Gardner glares at Seagrave. His mood is a bar graph of ascending angriness.

'Was that you Stuart?'

'Sorry Sir?' The whole group is now sniggering and staring at him.

'Stuart Seagrave, was it you who made that disgusting noise?'

'Well...' Seagrave is peering shame-faced from under the brim of his sun hat.

'Was that you?' Mr Gardner's rage is now close to the top of the x-axis.

'Well, I didn't mean to – '

'You filthy, disgusting boy. Get over there now.'

'But – '

'Don't answer me back. Go and stand over there.' Mr Gardner points at a spot on the far side of the clearing on the top of the cliff. 'I won't tolerate that kind of filthy behaviour. Go and stand over there until I tell you otherwise.'

Seagrave's sun hat has done nothing to protect him from the red face he is now wearing. He limps slowly and dejectedly towards the point at the far side of the clifftop parking area where Mr Gardner had indicated.

'And I don't want any messing about like that from the rest of you either.'

'There you are, Sir,' Martin continues. 'That's exactly the kind of thing Gunson and I are having to put up with, sharing a room with Seagrave.'

'All right Martin, that's enough.'

'But it's just not right, Sir. How are we supposed to do our work properly when we're having to put up with Seagrave's farting arse the whole time? What chance do any of us have with that going on? You talk about the threats to the climate and air pollution and acid rain and all that. And what the causes of it are. Well the cause of it all is right there: Seagrave's arse. No wonder the Earth is in peril. What chance do we have of fixing the ozone layer when you've got Seagrave's farting arse blowing a hole in it?'

There is much hilarity from the rest of the group. Mr Gardner tells Martin to hush up but Martin now has an audience and is warming to his subject. As soon as the teachers' backs are turned he continues. 'You see what I have to share a room with? It's like sleeping next to the fallout from an atomic bomb. Its output is measured in kiloton yield. Jesus, you could use it as a weapon. Yes, I can see it now: Britain is at war and the order goes out – deploy Seagrave's arse against the enemy. It's the ultimate deterrent, an agent of chemical warfare, a weapon of mass destruction. You've all heard about the SALT talks, yeah? Strategic Arms Limitation Talks. The Americans and Russians sat round a table talking about their stockpile of weapons. They're not talking about cruise missiles and nuclear bombs and stuff. No, they're talking about Seagrave's arse and who has control of it. Hey, what are you all laughing for? It's not funny. If Seagrave's arse were to fall into unfriendly hands the consequences for world peace would be catastrophic...'

Martin, after all this ribaldry, is not so smiley-faced a few minutes later when we have to begin our next field trip task. The banishment of Seagrave, coupled with both teachers currently standing close by and watching us, means that Martin has to actually get on and do some work instead of loafing about.

This task requires us to dig pieces of shale and slate out of the ground and then use a compass to note the orientation of the long axis. It occurs to me that, once these pieces of stone have been dug out you can't really put them back. And the area we are working in does not seem to be infinitely large. Shouldn't we be taking a bit more care and leaving some of this stuff for the benefit of future generations? To be fair to Martin though, he does seem to be getting on with the job more enthusiastically than I thought he would. Digging up and plundering bits of rock that have lain undisturbed for thousands of years – that seems to come to him very naturally.

A few yards away Rob Northwood and Paul Armstrong are meant to be doing the same task. But instead they start amusing themselves by taking the shales they have dug up, chucking them over the side of the cliff and watching where they land. They start with individual pieces before progressing onto huge handfuls of rock. Once they have mined out all the shale pieces they start throwing off anything else that they find nearby. A small tree is pulled up and that too is sent tumbling over the edge to its destruction.

There has been a lot of discussion in our geography lessons about the ways that wind and sea can shape our coastlines, but from what I'm seeing here it's the effects of a geography field trip on coastal erosion that is the more serious threat. In fact, burrowing out all these bits of shale has left the surface of the cliff top very uneven. I've already noticed Linda Sterling trip up on one of the holes. Someone could really do their leg in up here if they're not careful.

Another ten minutes or so pass and all the measuring and recording is complete. I'm just collecting up my stuff when Julie Whitworth and Linda Sterling wander over to me.

'How's it going, Adam?' asks Julie. They are both giggling.

'Yeah, fine.' I reply.

Why are they talking to me? Girls never talk to me.

'Did you get some good results then?'

'Yes I think so.'

'That's good. We'll share ours with you later then, yeah?'

'Yes okay.'

They walk off, both still giggling. What was that all about? Mr Gardner had said that each individual study group will need to share their own data with the others later on, so we can form a more complete analysis in our write-ups. But why has Julie Whitworth just come up to me and asked me about that. It's almost like she was looking for an excuse to talk to me.

By the way, in case you've been wondering why the two teachers didn't step in and stop Rob Northwood and Paul Armstrong from destroying the clifftop, it's because about twenty minutes ago they had driven away in both minibuses. They now return in just one of them. Mr Gardner tells us what the plan is for the rest of the day: rather than drive back to Shore Haven we are all going to walk there along the coastal path. The teachers have parked one of the minibuses at the hotel and will use that later to retrieve the one they are leaving here.

We are told we can put our bags in the minibus to save carrying them. I place my own bag in the back and decide to leave my anorak in there too. It's a hot day with no threat of rain so I won't be needing it. I've never liked that anorak. It's a brownish beige colour with a plastic zip, not at all smart or cool. My mum bought it for me from the Great Universal Stores catalogue. I only brought it with me because it's the one waterproof coat I have.

Mr Gardner feels that Seagrave has served sufficient penance for his apparent rudeness and he allows him to re-join the rest of the group. Once we have consumed our packed lunches the teachers lock up the minibus and we begin the walk. It's a narrow path so we are having to go single file.

After ten minutes of walking, the wide beach is behind us and we are heading towards a rocky headland. The tide is now coming in and the waves are crashing at the base of the cliff below us. It is an awe-inspiring sight. Striding just in front of me are Julie Whitworth and the other girls. They are regularly giggling and turning their heads in my direction and giggling some more. What's going on here? Does one of them fancy me? Do all of them fancy me, maybe? I come to the conclusion that walking along a clifftop path by the sea on a lovely day like this is a very fine way to spend an afternoon.

Chapter 6

It's four hours later and I am back in the hotel room. My body is exhausted, my limbs are aching and my feet are killing me. Mr Gardner's plan of walking back along the coastal path has turned out to be an absolute nightmare.

The walk was seven miles long. Seven miles, trekking along a rocky clifftop path with layers of gorse and bracken intruding on either side. I should have been doing this walk with Roz. If Roz had been there maybe I would have already asked her out by now. If Roz had been there maybe we would already be boyfriend and girlfriend by now. Maybe we would be walking along the clifftop together, hand in hand maybe, arm in arm maybe, stealing ourselves behind that wind-shaped tree for a secret kiss, maybe. But no, Roz hadn't been there and, obviously, none of those things had happened.

I suppose the walk had started off nicely enough. A warm, sunny day, lots of smiling faces, no more work to do, just a nice stroll taking in the picturesque landscape.

But then one hour would pass, and then another, and then another, and we seemed no closer to the end of it.

Gemma Thorneycroft was the first to complain, 'Sir, how much further is it?' More of us quickly joined in with the same chorus but Mr Gardner just told us to keep going. And so we continued, and what had started as a bright blue sky above us slowly became a bitter, scorching sun and with every passing step the sublime coastal scenery changed by degrees into a cruel seascape of despair. And bit by bit, the laughs and giggles turned into tired, weary, increasingly desperate moans. Every so often the path would approach a headland and you'd be thinking we were close to the end, just get round this last headland and the Shore Haven beach and the hotel would roll into view. But no, we would pass around the headland and there would be no beach and no hotel, just miles of more cliff and more path with another headland in the far distance offering us the same hope. And we'd get to that headland and it would be the same thing, our hopes of an end to it all dashed to oblivion just like the sea was dashing against those lifeless rocks at the base of the cliffs below us.

It's four hours later and Martin Vickers and I have finally limped back into our hotel room. And one thing I now know for certain. Green Flash trainers may look sharp, they may look cool, but they are totally unsuited for any kind of long-distance hiking.

After getting back to the hotel we had to wait a further half an hour, while the teachers retrieved the other minibus, before we could get our bags and coats back. With that now done I am finally able to crash out on the bunk bed and peel the trainers and socks from my throbbing feet. The soles of both feet are covered in blisters. They are shockingly painful.

Martin isn't saying anything but surely he must be aching as much as I am. I can't believe that those army boots of his would have been at all comfortable. I can't believe his feet have survived the ordeal better than mine. And then in comes Stuart Seagrave, his rucksack trailing mournfully behind him.

'Here he is,' laughs Martin, 'Britain's most powerful wind turbine.'

'Sod off, Vickers.' Seagrave is angry and tired and is also showing the ill effects from hours of walking. The shoes he has on are a cruddy-looking pair of docksiders; his feet must be in an even worse state than mine after trudging seven miles in those. 'That was so embarrassing, Mr Gardner treating me like that. Oh, and thanks. Yeah, thanks a lot for dobbing me in.'

'Oh stop belly-aching. Everyone knew it was you.'

Seagrave huffily dumps his rucksack onto the bed. 'It wasn't my fault. I can't help it if the food they serve here plays havoc with my bowels.'

'We all had the same food. You're the only one who had a force nine gale blowing out of his arse.'

'It's so unfair. Mr Gardner humiliating me in front of everyone. I can't help it if my body has to make natural noises.'

'Natural? Seagrave, there is nothing natural about your arse. That fart was like a tectonic event. It could have caused the whole cliff to collapse. We could've all died.'

'Yes all right. Will you stop going on about it please.'

'Is there nothing you can do to stop it? Can't you stick something up there like a plug or a peg or something?'

'WILL YOU PLEASE STOP GOING ON ABOUT MY ARSE!'

'Alright Seagrave, keep your rag on. I'm only trying to be helpful. All I'm saying is that you obviously have a problem with farting and an anal peg may be the answer. Hey, what's this?'

A piece of paper has been left on the small table next to the double bed. Martin picks it up and reads it:

> *Folks. Please be careful about walking mud from the beach into the hotel. One of you in this room has trodden mud from the beach into the carpet. We have cleaned it up for you this time but won't be doing it again. If you get more mud on the carpets please come down to the reception desk and we will give you some cleaning things so you can clean it up yourselves. Many thanks.*

Martin looks at both Seagrave and me. 'It's one of you that's done this. I didn't leave the hotel yesterday. It must be one of you two.'

'It wasn't me,' says Seagrave.

'It wasn't me,' I say. What is Seagrave like? I know full well it was him. I saw him do it. I really should have said something when I saw the mud on the carpet yesterday.

'Unbelievable,' says Martin. 'Anyway, I'm out of here.'

'What?' says Seagrave. 'Where are you going?'

'Somewhere other than where you are.'

'What about the writing up of today's field work? Mr Gardner told us to make a start on it before dinner.'

'Bollocks to that,' says Martin. 'I'm off to find some action.' And with that he walks out of the room leaving me and Seagrave alone.

Like I said before, Martin Vickers is not someone that I have mixed with much since our days at primary school. While at Tangley Wood I did share an English lesson with him during the second and third years, but otherwise we appear to have travelled down different paths. The recent time I've spent in his company has been a bit of an eye-opener.

Martin has certainly changed a bit since primary school. His main interests now seem to be the British Army, war comics and heavy metal music. To be honest, I'm not entirely sure what to make of him. He has a bullet-headed hair style, close to a skinhead cut but a few steps removed. And, whilst he seems comfortable in the company of guys like Rob Northwood, I don't think he's a fully paid up, card-carrying member of the gang. I remember once seeing an interview with Sting where he was talking about his music. He was asked whether The Police were a punk band and he had said no, they weren't a punk band but they did want to play music for the punks. And I think it's a similar thing with Martin – he's not a skinhead himself but he's able to hang out with skins and thugs and bond with them in ways that the rest of us wouldn't dare to.

In primary school (and prior to my playing field maiming) I used to sit at the same work table as Martin. That earlier, more cherubic version of Martin had had longer hair and was known for being something of a storyteller. In particular, I remember one morning where the teacher had told us all to write a story on any topic we liked and Martin had come up with a rather bold idea involving time travel.

'The lavatory in my home is a time machine,' he had explained. 'I go in the lavatory and sit on the seat and flush the handle and it takes me back in time to 1945 and there I am, fighting the Nazis.'

Bold and imaginative, I think you would agree. However, excited though he was with his marvellous story, he had found it hard to get going because the eight-year-old Martin didn't know how to spell the word 'lavatory'. So he had gone up to the teacher and asked her to give the spelling to him (it was customary, if you didn't know how to spell a word, to go up and ask the teacher to write it for you in your exercise book).

Martin had then come back and proceeded to make a start on his epic tale.

'Hey,' I pointed out, 'that's not "lavatory", that's "laboratory".'

'What?'

'"Laboratory". The place where scientists work. You've asked for the wrong word.'

'I asked her for "lavatory".'

'She must have misheard you.'

I suppose it's easy to see how it would have happened. If you tell the teacher you're writing a story about a time machine then 'laboratory' is a more obvious word to be using than 'lavatory'.

'Aren't you gonna go back up and ask her to spell "lavatory"?'

'Nah, I think I'll leave it. Just change the story to me making a time machine in a laboratory. Me fighting the Nazis is still the main bit, anyway.'

And so it was that his story ended up following a somewhat different road to that which he had originally planned. Which was a shame, as I would have liked to have known more about Martin's time-travelling toilet. I guess there are some stories that are never meant to be told.

As I say, I'm still not sure how I feel about Martin Vickers. I am sure how I feel about Stuart Seagrave though. Stuart Seagrave is a pain. With Martin gone we start sifting through our notes from the day. For some reason

Seagrave thinks he is now in charge. He starts bossing me around, barking commands at me like 'Adam, where are you with the pebble chart?' and 'Adam, where is your till fabric data, so I can start plotting it.'

This micro-management goes on for about fifteen minutes and then there is a knock on the door. I recall how Julie Whitworth had spoken to me earlier and I wonder if it might be her, come to share her figures. I move swiftly to the door and open it. But it isn't Julie, it's Isaac, here on a similar mission. I don't really want to have yet another insane conversation with Isaac so I let Seagrave deal with him instead.

No sooner has Isaac finished and gone than we are interrupted again, this time with no knock. Martin has returned. 'Hey Gunson,' he calls to me, 'we need you downstairs in the games room.'

'What?' Seagrave protests. 'No. He can't go.'

'We need his help with something. It won't take a minute.'

'No, absolutely not.' Seagrave is adamant. 'Adam and I are both busy. Busy doing the work you're meant to be doing as well, actually.'

'Hey Seagrave, are you okay?'

'What? No of course I'm not okay. We've got serious work that we're supposed to be getting on with here but all you care about is messing around. Why would I be okay about that?'

'No,' says Martin, 'what I meant was, you seem to be having a nosebleed.'

'What?' Sure enough, a trickle of blood has started to emerge from Seagrave's right nostril. He dabs his nose with his left hand and looks at the blood on his fingers. 'Oh bloody hell. Bloody, bloody hell.' He scurries off into the bathroom.

'He shouldn't get so upset about stuff,' says Martin. 'Right, come on.'

'Shouldn't we check he's okay first?' I ask.

'Nah, he'll be fine. Come on.'

To be fair, Seagrave does have a bit of a history with nosebleeds. I remember him having one once during a French lesson when he got stressed about the concept of pain-au-chocolat.

I'm curious as to what it is Martin wants me for. Slipping on my moccasins I am immediately reminded of how sore my feet still are but, undeterred, I leave the room and follow him down the stairs.

Martin leads me through the lobby towards a door at the back of the bar. This door opens onto the games room, a small, separate area at the rear of the hotel. I had discovered this games room yesterday when I had been checking the place out. It does not appear to be part of the original building but more of a later add-on, constructed from yellow-painted concrete. The room is lit by some grimy, block glass windows high up on the walls – the kind of windows you get in a public toilet. In the middle of the room is an old pool table with a faded blue baize. Dotted round the walls are a Space Invaders cabinet and a couple of video game tables.

The room is busy: Chas Browning and Colin Winchester are sat around one of the game tables and Rob Northwood and Paul Armstrong are stood next to the pool table, apparently waiting for us. Rob Northwood has one of the pool cues in hand and is brandishing it in a way that complements his usual, threatening demeanour. Julie and Linda are also present, seemingly as spectators. There is no pool game currently in progress, the balls are all still inside the table.

'Okay,' explains Martin, 'the issue we have is that to get the balls out you need to put in 20p.'

'Oh, I respond. 'So do you just want me to give you 20p then?'

'No,' says Paul Armstrong. 'We don't want your money.'

'No. What we have discovered,' Martin continues, 'is that you don't need to put any money in to get the balls out. See here...' He indicates the side of the pool table where there is a hole, about five inches square, next to the window displaying the balls inside. There must once have been a panel of some kind covering it but that is now gone, leaving a visible open hole with rough edges. 'If you put your hand in here,' Martin goes on, 'and reach inside you can twist the rack and get all the balls out without having to pay. That's where you come in.'

'How do you mean?'

'We've each tried it but our wrists are all too thick. We can't get them through the hole. That's why we thought of you.'

'Me?'

'Yeah. We need someone with thin, skinny, weakling arms to reach inside and get to the mechanism.'

'And you thought of me?'

'Yeah. Well it was either you or Seagrave. But there's no point asking Pipecleaner Boy, that bastard would never agree to it.'

'I-I'm not sure,' I respond thinly. 'What if someone sees us? One of the hotel staff.'

'Oh come on Gunson, join in. It'll be fine. No one's watching.'

'Yeah come on Gunson, don't be a twat.'

'Just get on with it. Come on, it's easy. It'll only take you a few seconds.'

'We'll let you have a game as well.'

Rob Northwood and Paul Armstrong are both urging me to do it and Julie and Linda are now joining in as well.

'Come on Adam.'

'Yeah come on Adam. Help the boys out.'

I'm really not at all comfortable about doing this but I think it's the smiles of the two girls that finally persuade me. 'Alright then,' I say, 'what do I need to do?'

'Just put your left arm through that hole.'

'You might want to remove your watch first.'

That sounds fair enough. I slip off my watch, crouch down next to the pool table and reach into the hole. 'What if my arm gets stuck?' I ask.

'It won't get stuck. Just get on with it.'

Tentatively I push my left arm all the way in right up to the shoulder. I must look like a farm vet assisting with a difficult birth. I'm conscious that everyone in the room has now assembled to watch me do this thing. Among the crowd of bodies clustered round me I catch sight of some yellow jumpers – a few of the students from that other school have also come in and joined the audience.

'What do I do now?'

'Feel around inside until you can find the rack with the balls on it. That's it. Now try twisting the rack up and to the right. It should rotate and all the balls should then come out.'

'It's not moving.'

'Twist it harder.'

I struggle, my arm and hand wrestling deep inside the table's inner workings. Then suddenly there is a metallic spring-like sound, followed by a series of clunks, and that's it. I have successfully delivered the pool balls – they all roll through to the opening at the end of the table.

'Nice one!'

There follows a round of applause with cheers and laughter from everyone that watched me do this. And I'm thinking, wow, this is nice. This must be what it feels like to be popular. But my joy is short-lived as, when I turn my head, I see the crowd separate to reveal a lone figure stood at the back, glaring at me. It's the hotel manager.

I recognise the hotel manager from yesterday – he had been stood behind the desk in the foyer when our room keys were being handed out. The hotel manager is a large, muscular man with a thick neck, a head like a bowling ball and a face like a knuckle. He's wearing a short-sleeved polo shirt and the tattoos on his bare arms suggest he might be ex-military. He stares first at me (I am now rigid with fear, my arm still wedged inside the pool table), then at everyone else in turn, then at me again. 'Alright lads?' he says in a slow, accusatory manner.

'Yes fine thanks,' Martin steps in. '20p for a game of pool. Very reasonable.'

The hotel manager is still staring hard at me. I'm expecting him to come over, grab me by the collar and throw me out into the road. But instead he just shakes his head, the slow headshake of disappointment, before turning and walking away.

I retrieve my arm from the pool table and hastily get to my feet. I can feel myself shaking from what has just gone down.

With the drama over, everyone returns to what they were doing before. Julie and Linda have now moved over to the video game table where Chas Browning is giving a masterclass on how to play Asteroids. I was expecting to at least get some sort of thank you from Martin and the others, considering what I've just put myself through. But no, Martin just gathers all the pool balls, racks them up and begins a game with Rob

Northwood. A couple of the yellow jumpers from the other school join them at the table. 'Nice trick getting the balls out like that,' one of them says. 'Okay if I play the winner?'

I don't really want to stick around here. I'm obviously in trouble with the authorities now and I sense that, in the near future, I will be having a difficult conversation with Mr Gardner. Jesus, what have I got myself into? It would have been easier just to have given them the 20p. I just want to get back up to the room and try not to think about it. So I turn to head out and suddenly find myself face to face with a girl.

'Wow!' says the girl, 'that was amazing!'

'Sorry?'

'What you did there. The way you just faced him down like that. That manager guy. Like, wow, he had you caught red handed and you just stared back at him and said nothing until he went away. That was incredible. That's one of the most amazing things I've ever seen.'

'Oh,' I say. 'Right. Thanks.'

She is one of the students from that other school and has the yellow jumper with 'Kimble College' written across her chest. 'Here,' she says, 'you left this over on the table.' She hands my watch back to me.

'Oh. Thanks.'

'You're not playing pool yourself then?'

'Err, no. No, pool's not really my game. I'm more of a...' My eyes happen upon the video game cabinet next to the wall. '... more of a Space Invaders guy.'

'Cool,' says the girl. 'Me too. Come on, I'll give you a game.'

An instant later I am standing in front of the Space Invaders cabinet with this girl next to me. In truth I don't know much about Space Invaders and have only played it a couple of times before now. I put my 10p in the coin slot and then proceed to lose all three of my lives in fast succession. It's an embarrassing performance and I'm fully expecting the girl to tell me so.

But instead she says, 'Hey look, you've got a high score.'

The machine tells me that I do indeed have a high score. However this is because there are only three other scores listed on the screen. The game has obviously not seen much use of late. The current top score is showing as 6,230, achieved by someone called Stiffy. My score is 60.

'Are you going to record your score?' she asks. I'm struggling to identify her accent. Liverpool? Manchester?

'No' I reply. 'I think I'll leave it. It's not one of my best scores.'

'To get a better score you need to hit those flying saucers that go across the top of the screen. You get bonus points for those.'

'Yes I know. It's difficult to hit those though.'

'Difficult? What makes you say that?'

'Sorry?'

'What makes hitting the flying saucers difficult?'

'It's... it's tricky. Because they move so fast and those other alien things are in the way.'

'Okay then, let me try.' She puts her own 10p in the coin slot and starts playing. Annoyingly, she seems to be quite good at it. Her slim fingers dance assuredly over the joystick and buttons. As well as shooting out most of the descending ranks of invaders and nimbly avoiding the incoming missiles she also manages to hit a couple of the flying saucers.

I watch her while she focuses her attention on the game. She has fine, pointy features and rich, brown hair in a ponytail tied high up on the back of her head. And there is something striking about the way her face is lit up by the glow from the console screen. By the time she loses the last of her three lives her score is standing at 1,530. 'There you go,' she says, smiling. 'That wasn't so difficult.'

'You got a high score,' I point out, 'Are you going to record it?'

'No,' she says. 'Not one of my best scores. Anyway –'

She is interrupted by someone calling out to her. It's another Kimble College girl, shouting from over by the entrance. 'Jen, Come on, we'll be late.'

'Sorry,' she says. 'Got to go. Have fun!' She smiles at me and then turns to leave. 'Oh, by the way.' She turns back to me. 'It looks like you've caught a bit of sunburn. You might want to do something about that.' I watch her as she follows the other girl out, her black Converse trainers skipping across the concrete floor.

I decide to not play any more Space Invaders. I don't think it's the game for me. I've just been humiliated at it by a girl, I don't have any more 10p's and it's unlikely that I'll be challenging Stiffy's high score any time soon. I glance around the room. Martin and Rob Northwood's pool game has just come to an end, seemingly due to Martin having fouled the eight ball. One of the Kimble College guys, who apparently is called Hughie, is offering the winner a game. They don't need my help anymore releasing the balls as Hughie is lean enough and skinny enough to do that trick himself. Julie and Linda are still watching Chas Browning save the universe.

What was it that girl just said? That I had caught a bit of sunburn? I touch my fingers to my face and immediately sense that familiar sunburn sting. There's a gent's toilet in the hotel bar area. I leave the games room and dash in there to use the mirror. Bloody hell, my face looks absolutely scorched. Yes, today I was walking for four hours under the blazing Pembrokeshire sun with no skin protection and tomorrow I'm going to be looking like a lobster thermidor. That's just terrific, that is.

Chapter 7

I spend the rest of the day convinced that, at any moment, Mr Gardner will accost me, drag me aside and administer punishment for my criminal doings with the pool table. I'm fully believing that the hotel manager has informed him of my acts and that he'll be coming for me some time soon. It's a worrying prospect. I've seen what he's like when he's upset and I really do not want to be on the wrong end of that beard.

When we go down to have our dinner (this evening's meal is some kind of meat stew) I'm bracing myself for Mr Gardner hauling me out in front of everyone and chastising me. But it doesn't happen. Mr Gardner gives the same speech he did last night about not tolerating any clowning around or stupid antics (this seems to be directed mostly at Seagrave) but apart from that, nothing.

After dinner when we are back in the room there are a couple of knocks at the door but it's just the others from our group, first Julie and then Chas, come to share their data. Later, Mr Gardner does knock on the door and when I see him there I am literally bracing myself for the worst. But again, nothing happens. Seagrave, following the events of the morning, is desperate to try and get back into Mr Gardner's favour. He proceeds to suck up to him and proudly shows off our completed work. All those pebble measurements are neatly piled up into bar charts and the till fabric analysis is keenly plotted out on a compass rose diagram. Mr Gardner seems happy with that and leaves.

I must give some credit to Seagrave actually. He is a pain to be with but, with his direction, we did manage to get all that work written up in good time. If it had been left to just me and Martin I don't think we would have got anything done.

So I seem to have avoided Mr Gardner's wrath for this evening at least. Have I got away with it completely? That's doubtful. Will my reckoning come sometime tomorrow? Probably. But at least I have survived long enough to see another sunrise.

Of course, Seagrave has already had it in the neck from Mr Gardner today. Did that outburst of flatulence really warrant the punishment that was doled out to him? I wouldn't have thought so myself. I guess Mr Gardner is one of those teachers who like to stamp their authority on the class and keep a tight rein on things. And I'm not saying that is necessarily a bad thing. No, not at all. In fact, I've always been more comfortable in lessons where the teacher is in control. And, generally speaking, I've got on well with most of my teachers most of the time. But one thing I have found out during my time at Tangley Wood School is that, if a teacher has a bad reputation they have it for a reason, and any evidence to the contrary should be treated with caution. I learnt that with Mr Charlton, my third year science teacher.

When, at the start of the third year, I first learnt that I would be having Mr Charlton for science, I confess that I was anxious. Everyone who had had classes with him before called him 'that nutter Charlton' who was always screaming and shouting and carrying on during the lessons. I had therefore gone into that first lesson with some trepidation.

Despite my concerns, it had appeared to go okay. I remember the subject of the lesson being quite difficult, something to do with measuring wave frequency and amplitude and that kind of stuff, but it all seemed to pass without any drama or tension. He had said a few words about his expectations regarding homework but nothing more serious than that. And I left thinking, this Mr Charlton, he seems all right. A harmless, amiable old guy, I thought. Not the crazed lunatic everyone seems to say he is, I thought.

I was, of course, wrong.

I went along to the next lesson, the following week, not thinking there would be anything to concern me. I had done the homework and handed it in on time.

There was nothing for me to worry about, or so I thought.

We all sat at our desks and, right from the very start, you could sense things were different to last week. There was a bad atmosphere draped over the room like a threatening storm cloud. And there was Mr Charlton, stood by his desk and glaring at us from behind his National Health glasses. His face was dark pink, glistening with rage and contempt.

He started shouting at us. 'Did I not tell you all, last week,' he began, belligerently, 'that the one thing I won't tolerate is homework not being done? Did I not say that?'

On the table in front of him was a pile of our exercise books. He got up from his chair, picked up the book at the top of the pile and walked over to us.

There was I thinking, oh dear, someone's in for it. And then I looked up and saw that he was standing right in front of me.

'You. Adam Gunson. Where's your homework?'

And it was my exercise book that he had in his hand. He slapped it down hard on the desk in front of me.

'Sorry Sir?'

'You've handed this in with no homework in it.'

'What do you mean?'

'Where's your homework, Gunson?'

I should say at this point that I was not a kid who was regularly in trouble for not doing homework. This was not the kind of teacher-pupil interaction that I was used to. But I could feel that all the other eyes in the room were now on me, sensing my impending doom.

'My homework? It-it's there', I said, anxiously pointing.

'Don't treat me like a fool. That isn't the homework. That's the work we did in the lesson.'

'N-no,' I said, 'that's the homework. The work we did in the lesson is here.' And I turned the book to the previous page to show him. Mind you, I say that calmly enough now. I had been fairly sure my homework had been in my exercise book, but I was in such a state of fear that, at the time, I was beginning to doubt whether it was actually still there.

Mr Charlton looked at it. He turned back and forth between the two pages. 'But this is written out in the same format as the work from the lesson.'

'Yes. I followed the same method for the homework as you showed us for the example we did in class.'

I mean, come on. That's the way, isn't it? The teacher shows you how to solve the problem and you then apply the same process in a similar way for the homework. Yes?

Mr Charlton looked at it again. Eventually he said, grudgingly, 'Well, okay, I suppose it deserves some kind of mark.' And he walked back to the front of the room and continued with the rest of the lesson.

I did that homework. I may not have done it well, but I did it. And I handed it in on time. I never did get an apology. Mr Charlton had said it deserved marking but I never did get it marked, because that would have meant going up to him at the end of the lesson which was the most terrifying thing I could imagine.

I don't think I am someone who typically bears a longstanding grudge, but that wounded me. It wounded me much more than having a piece of wood stabbed in my shin ever did. That man did me wrong. In the weeks that followed, those science lessons would invariably descend into the same kind of crazy shouting and accusations, though thankfully the wrath of Charlton was usually directed at others rather than me.

I had told Derek about how I reckoned Mr Charlton was the worst teacher I'd ever had. In response, Derek had said *his* worst teacher was Mr Enfield, the art teacher. 'I used to enjoy art, used to be quite good at it,' Derek had explained, 'and I thought art lessons would be learning about drawing and how to use oil paints and watercolours and stuff like that.

'But what did Enfield do? He got us to draw pictures of shoes. Not using pencils or crayons or anything sensible like that. No, he had us drawing pictures of shoes using biros. And then, after telling us all how piss-poor our drawings were, he made us do them again. And then again, until a whole term had gone by. And it's not like he gave us any help or demonstrations or anything, he just told us to get on with it and then gave us rubbish marks for our efforts.

'Of course, you know what the truth is? The truth is that the man isn't a proper art teacher at all. He's a photography teacher. Photography is the only thing he knows how to do. But he has to teach art as well because it was in the job description.

'Imagine that. All those times judging our drawings, telling us how rubbish they were, and he couldn't even do it himself. No wonder he never did any demonstrations in the class. He's an art teacher but he can't draw.

'And have you seen what he wears? That tartan jacket. And those shoes. Those awful, chronic, green shoes. How can a man who claims to know about art wear shoes like that? I used to enjoy art but Enfield killed it for me. He made me draw pictures of shoes with a biro, while he himself knows nothing about art and he knows nothing about shoes.'

Stuart Seagrave keeps a diary. It's an A4-sized notebook with a brown paper cover and the word 'PRIVATE' boldly stencilled on the front. I'm lying in my bunk bed watching him while he writes in it. He wrote in it yesterday at about the same time and he's writing in it again now, sat up on the bed with his back against the headboard. He is careful though to only write in it at times when Martin Vickers is not in the room. 'Don't tell Vickers about my diary,' he warns me. 'He'll only try to steal it and read it and make fun of me. And I don't want that. And I don't want you reading it either.'

When he's not writing in his diary he packs it in the bottom of his suitcase which he then locks with a key. I wonder what he's writing in it. Does it contain a load of flowery stuff about his feelings and emotions? Has he catalogued a detailed description of the seismic farting episode from up on the cliff top earlier? Or is his diary just a bare, sober record of the facts of the day? It's more likely to be the latter. Somehow I can't picture him as a person who writes about his emotions. He needn't worry, I have no intention of reading his diary. I'm sure there's nothing in Seagrave's diary that could be of any interest to me.

I've never kept a diary myself. I do sometimes think about writing, though. About writing a novel. If I wrote a novel that was really successful and made a lot of money then I wouldn't need to get a proper job when I leave school. Yes, that would be good. The only problem is that I don't like writing very much. It's like doing homework. I always find it to be such a chore.

Which reminds me. I need to get a postcard to send to my mum and dad before the end of the week. I promised I would send them one. Writing postcards is such a drag though. And what am I going to tell them? What's happened to me so far on this trip? I'm sharing a room with two lunatics, my feet are covered with blisters, I've got sunstroke, by this time tomorrow the skin will be peeling off my face like a leper, I'm in trouble with the hotel management for interfering with a pool table and I've been humiliated at Space Invaders by a girl called Jen from another school. Having a lovely time.

Chapter 8

Another hour has passed and I've made no further progress with those essays. I also seem to have eaten all the biscuits. I'm not sure how or when that happened but the empty carton is testament to the fact that they are now all gone.

Maybe I should give up on the marking and watch TV for a bit. Where's the TV guide? I pick it up and take a look at what's on right now. Channel Four are showing a Peter Sellers film called *After the Fox*. Do I want to watch that? Hmm, not sure. I've also still got those films that I recorded a while ago. *Fight Club* and *The Usual Suspects*. I suppose I could watch one of those.

The thing is though, ever since the lockdown started all I ever seem to do is watch TV. Stay in the house all day and watch TV. Life is a bit rubbish at the moment, isn't it? I've had a couple of years of getting used to living on my own but, even so, being stuck inside like this and never seeing another human soul, it's a pretty desperate situation.

Don't you sometimes wish you had a time machine? Don't you wish you could escape from the world we live in now and travel back to somewhere else? Back to some happier, sunnier time? Or back to a time where you could put right that thing that went wrong, or do that thing that you should have done but didn't?

Hey, I'm not fussy. Any time machine would do...

It's the second morning of the geography field trip and today is shopping survey day. The time is ten o'clock and the green minibus has just dropped us off at a car park in Milford Haven. I am there with Martin Vickers and Stuart Seagrave (you probably guessed that much). Also with us are Gemma Thorneycroft and Rachel Barrett, dressed in the same jumpsuits they were wearing on Monday. The rest of our group have been taken in the second minibus to two other local towns, Haverfordwest and Fishguard, so they can do similar surveys there.

I'm actually surprised at how well I slept last night. I must have been tired after all that walking. I thought I was going to spend the whole time tossing and turning, worrying about that business with the hotel manager. But I slept well. Not even Seagrave's constant wheezing seemed to disturb me. I was only briefly roused at around eleven, when Martin had come sneaking back to the room. In the morning he told us he had been to the pub with Rob Northwood. Seagrave told Martin he was crazy to be taking such a risk and pointed out that if Mr

Gardner had caught them they would almost certainly be sent home. But Martin said he wasn't fazed by that.

All through the morning I'd still been expecting to be in trouble with Mr Gardner. I had seen the hotel manager, stood at the reception desk, when we came down for breakfast. I looked at him. He looked at me. I smiled weakly at him. He didn't smile at me. He just slowly shook that bowling ball head of his, like he had the day before. Surely he was going to complain about me to Mr Gardner now, wasn't he? Well seemingly not. Mr Gardner had said nothing over breakfast and he said nothing in the minibus during the eight mile trip to Milford Haven. Maybe I really had got away with it.

The minibus drives off and we are left to make our own way out of the car park. We haven't been given any maps or anything but fairly soon we find ourselves walking through into what appears to be the centre of the town.

'Right,' says Gemma, 'let's go check out the shops.'

Rachel mumbles in agreement but Seagrave, of course, protests at the very suggestion. 'We've got work to do,' he pleads with them. 'The reason we here is to do a shopping survey.'

'Forget that,' says Gemma. 'We're not here for the shopping survey, we're here for the shopping. Come on Rachel.' And the two girls flounce away down the street.

'Yeah, come on,' says Martin, 'let's check the place out.'

'No,' says Seagrave firmly. 'Absolutely not. I'm not having a repeat of yesterday. We need to get this work done and we need to do it properly'

'Okay then.' Martin, suspiciously, appears to be in agreement. 'Why don't we split up? Stand outside different shops. That way we'll be able to question more people.'

'Yes, good idea,' Seagrave nods. 'Adam, why don't you set up further down the street while Vickers and I do the people up here?'

'Excellent,' says Martin. 'I'll head off the other way and do the same.'

'No you won't,' says Seagrave firmly. 'You're stopping here with me. Otherwise you'll just skive off and spend the whole morning doing nothing.'

'Oh, I see. It's like that, is it? You're letting Gunson go off on his own. D'you trust him not to skive off?'

'I don't trust him much either. But I trust him more than I trust you...'

The centre of Milford Haven consists of one shopping street that runs parallel to the harbour. I'm guessing it all mostly dates from some time in the 1960s and features concrete buildings with a couple of arcades on either side. Martin thinks that a spot outside a betting shop would be a good location but Seagrave overrules him. He makes them stand outside a building society instead. There is a branch of Woolworths further down the road and, having received Seagrave's blessing, I make my way along to it and position myself there.

I recall doing a similar survey for O Level geography in Woking a couple of years before. That had been a struggle – a cold Thursday afternoon with very few of the locals wanting to be helpful. At least today is a brighter day and quite warm, though not such a scorcher as yesterday had been. There are not many people about, though, and even fewer of them are coming in my direction. The Milford Haven Woolworths (a big, concrete-fronted edifice) must be the largest single shop in the town, but it isn't doing very much trade this morning.

I stand near the entrance to the store, clipboard in hand. Twenty minutes pass. During that time I get precisely two people to participate in my survey – an old lady who dresses a bit like my nan (shops here twice a week, uses public transport) and a grey haired man with a moustache and a jacketed dachshund (lives within walking distance, shops here only occasionally). This is ridiculous. I'm not getting anywhere. Is there a better spot to do this? I glance up and down the street. I'm not seeing any shops that look more promising than this one. There are not that many shops in this street at all, actually. Looking at the town as a whole, I'm guessing that Gemma and Rachel will find the place to be a disappointing shopping experience.

The road alongside Woolworths runs downhill towards the harbour. There's not much to see in that road, just houses and a fish and chip shop, so that doesn't look any more promising. And then on the far corner of that road I spot a sign bearing the familiar logo of the Mid-Westland Bank. A bank. Yes, that might be a better place to try. I leave the main street and wander down to see if I'm right.

I am not right, it turns out, because the bank is closed. It doesn't open on Wednesdays. Okay, so that's a bust then. And I'm just about to move off when I hear a voice calling to me.

'Hey! Pool table guy!'

It's that girl from yesterday. The one who thrashed me at Space Invaders.

'Hey, I thought it was you.'

'H-hi,' I mumble in response.

'What're you doing here?'

'Shopping survey.'

'Yes, I thought you might be, That clipboard you're clutching there is a bit of a giveaway. My lot are here doing the same thing.'

'There don't seem to be many people willing to take part though.'

'Yeah, it's a bit rubbish isn't it. Look, we're sat over here. Come and join us.'

The next thing I know I'm following her towards the other side of the road. She's wearing the same Wrangler jeans, trainers and jumper that she had on yesterday. Just across the road is a short wall with railings overlooking the harbour. On the left is a small area of grass with some benches. She leads me to one of the benches where another Kimble College girl is seated.

'Hey Leena, this is that guy I was telling you about. This is – sorry, I don't know your name.'

'Adam.'

'Adam. Hi. This is Leena. And I'm Jen.' She continues. 'Leena you should have seen this guy yesterday. It was incredible. This guy is fearless. The way he stared down the manager, you know, that miserable manager guy, the one who made us clean all the dirt off our boots...' Jen continues to relate the previous day's events, her face and hands coming alive as she speaks.

Leena, in contrast, seems to be far less impressed with my exploits. She has a face whose default setting appears to be 'stroppy.' She's tall and thin and has a bit of a goth look about her – straight, shoulder length dark hair, black-rimmed eyes, pale skin and dark lips. She's wearing black skinny jeans and DM boots that have been customised with spray paint – style choices that do not blend well with her yellow college jumper. I don't think she's a full goth. More like a novice goth. A goth in training, working her way towards the next level of darkness.

'Are you the one whose arse Jen whipped at Space Invaders?' Leena asks.

'Y-yes I am.'

'And did she tell you that we have a Space Invaders game in our college common room and she spends an hour every day playing it?'

'Shut up,' says Jen. 'That is an absolute lie. Okay, well maybe I do play on it most days but not for a whole hour. Half an hour, maybe. Forty minutes, tops. But yes, okay, I might have spent a tiny bit of time practising on it. Hey, guess what? Adam's been doing a shopping survey, same as us.'

'Really? Who'd have thought it?'

'He hasn't been able to get many responses though. We didn't get many either, did we?'

'Of course we didn't,' says Leena, testily. 'What d'you expect? People see you stood on the street holding a clipboard, wearing a college jumper and looking like a twat. They're obviously going to walk straight past.'

'I should be getting back to it,' I tell them. 'Our teacher will be upset if we go back without having many responses.'

'Here, let's see what you've got so far.' Jen takes my clipboard and starts scanning the sheet. 'These questions are almost the same as the ones we were asking. I know, why don't we fill it in for you with the answers we got?'

'I – I don't...' But before I can say more she has already fetched out her own notebook and has started copying across all the ticks and numbers onto my sheet. I should really be objecting to this behaviour. But instead I just sit there, watching her.

'There you go.' She passes the clipboard back to me. 'All sorted.'

'I thought you said you didn't get many responses.'

'Yes, well we didn't. We made up most of it. But it's fine. It all looks like it should do, see?'

'Oh, right.' I'm not sure whether to be concerned about this or not. Seagrave is not going to like it. Probably best not to tell him. Besides, there's something about Jen when she smiles at me that makes me unwilling to complain, 'Thanks,' I say.

'Right, that's all sorted now,' says Jen, 'so you're free to hang around with us for a bit. Looks like your sunburn has cleared up too.' She turns to Leena. 'Yesterday he had a really sunburnt face. He looks a lot better now, don't you think.'

'Yeah,' says Leena, cynically.

It's true though, my face has settled down a bit since yesterday. I stole some of Seagrave's moisturiser when I was in the bathroom, both last night and this morning, and it seems to have done the trick. (I was also able to mostly sort out the blisters on my feet with some help from Seagrave's nail scissors.)

'Thanks.' I continue, trying my best to think of something to talk about. 'So you're Jen then?'

'That's me.'

'Short for Jennifer?'

'No, just Jen.'

'Short for Jenny?'

'No.'

'What's it short for then?'

'Like I said, you can call me Jen.'

'Oh. Okay.' My eyes slide over towards Leena, who continues to regard me with disdain.

'Here,' says Jen, 'have one of these.'

She reaches into her tote bag. I'm thinking that she's going to offer me a cigarette. This could be awkward. I don't smoke, never have and ideally I don't want to be starting now. In my world cigarettes have always belonged in the domain of miscreants like Rob Northwood. But on the other hand, if Jen does offer me a cigarette there's a part of me that wouldn't want to refuse it. However, I'm relieved to see that what she pulls from her bag is not cigarettes, it's a narrow box containing a pack of biscuits.

'Here, take one.'

I thank her and take a biscuit from the pack. It's a type I have never seen before, a square, crisp biscuit with a thick layer of chocolate on one side overlapping the edges. The 'biscuit' side of the biscuit has some writing baked into it. Choco Leibniz.

'It's never too early in the day for one of these,' says Jen. 'They're my favourite biscuits. They're named after a German philosopher.'

'That's why she eats them,' says Leena. 'She thinks that if she eats enough of those biscuits it will make her better at philosophy.'

'Hey, shut up you.'

'Of course all they actually do is make her fat.'

'Is that so? In that case you won't be wanting any then?'

Leena moodily rolls her eyes and sticks her tongue out before taking one.

'She never says no to a biscuit,' says Jen, smiling.

I agree, they are indeed very nice biscuits. I consume mine in three bites but then feel slightly guilty when I see that Jen is taking time over hers, slowly nibbling at the chocolate edges first.

'I do like philosophy though,' Jen explains, 'so if there is any benefit to eating these biscuits then that would be good. I'm only doing geography as an extra subject to, you know, make up my A Levels. Philosophy is the thing that I'm really into. Politics and philosophy. Do you know anything about philosophy, Adam?'

I confess that I do not.

'At the moment we're doing Karl Marx. Marx's theory of history. You've heard of Karl Marx, yeah? He has this theory about history. Let me see if I can explain it. You know how, in a novel or a story, the things that happen are not just random things. They all happen for a reason. There is a writer, an author, who makes all the characters do certain things so the story unfolds the way it does. Well, Marx's theory is that the history of the world is the same. Rather than history just being a random series of events, Marx reckons that there is an underlying, controlling force, like the author of a novel. A force that has caused history to turn out the way it has.

'Do you know what that force is? No, not God or anything like that. No, Marx reckons the driving force of history is man's instinct to create things. He calls it the forces of production. His whole theory is based on the premise that man is, by nature, a being that produces things. Ha!' Jen breaks off with a laugh. She has finished nibbling the chocolate edges and is now starting work on the main biscuit. 'My philosophy teacher says that, if you get into an argument with a Marxist, one thing you can try is attacking Marx's initial premise. Kick away the initial premise of an argument and the rest will come tumbling down with it. I'm not sure how you would do that though, I don't think we've covered it in class yet. Actually, if I'm honest I'm not that fussed about the politics part, it's the philosophy part I'm most interested in. The politics is just an extra bit that happens to be included.'

'What she told me,' says Leena, 'is that she's studying philosophy because she wants to know about the soul. She's big on stuff about the soul. On account of her being a Catholic.'

'Hey, stop being mean.' Jen almost chokes on her last piece of biscuit. 'That's not right. Well okay, it's partly right. I do want to know about the soul. The mind. What consciousness is and where it comes from and all that. But we all want to know that, don't we? And anyway, my philosophy classes are fun. We have a really cool teacher. Philosophy is all about critical thinking and being curious about stuff and asking the sort of questions that teachers of other classes don't like you asking.'

'That's not what Hughie says,' says Leena. 'Hughie says that the only thing philosophy is good for is teaching you how to win an argument.'

'Well of course,' says Jen, 'Hughie would say that because Hughie is an idiot. But no, there's more to it than that. Studying philosophy isn't just about winning arguments. It's about stuff like...' I can see her thoughts reaching round to come up with something. 'I know. Adam, yesterday when you were playing Space Invaders you said you thought it was difficult.'

'Did I?'

'Yes you did. So what was it about Space Invaders that you thought was difficult?'

'I-I'm not sure. I suppose it's tricky getting that missile thing lined up so it fires in the right place every time.'

'Would you call it more or less difficult than say, digging a hole? Or putting a load of books in alphabetical order?'

'No, those things are easy.' I've no idea where this is going but I seem to be happy to just get pulled along with it.

'Okay,' Jen continues. Now, digging a hole requires physical effort. If you are a strong person you would probably find it easy. But if you were a weaker person you would probably find it difficult. And organising a load of books, yes that would probably take you a long time to do. But does taking a long time to do something mean that it is difficult? I don't think it does. Time consuming yes, but not necessarily difficult. But then again, if you were someone who didn't know the alphabet then you probably *would* find it difficult.

'I think what I'm trying to say, probably not very well, is that "difficulty" is a subjective thing. If you already have the knowledge or skill or strength to do a thing then it's easy, if you don't then it's difficult. Like with Space Invaders. You found it difficult and I found it easy but the only reason I found it easy was because I'd spent hours practising how to do it.'

She talks a lot, doesn't she? I'm quite liking listening to her though. And there's something about the way her face comes alive when she's telling me about this philosophy stuff, something that I can't help watching.

'Learning a skill like that requires a certain type of knowledge,' Jen continues. 'A type of knowledge that you can't get from reading a book. A type of knowledge that can't be conveyed by words. You have to learn it by doing it. By doing it and getting it wrong. Like riding a bike, for instance. Almost anyone is capable of riding a bike, it's just a case of mastering the necessary skill. Does that make sense?' She looks at me, still smiling. 'Hey, you don't say much, do you? Fearless but quiet. I like that in a man.'

'I'm not surprised he's quiet,' says Leena. 'When you start going on about philosophy there's no stopping you. No one else gets a look in.'

'Shut up you. Just because you're not interested doesn't mean that Adam isn't.'

'It's all a load of rubbish anyway. Philosophy, who cares about that? A bunch of old blokes talking about stuff that no one understands. What was that thing you were going on about the other day? Positive and negative freedom.'

'What about it?'

'That's just nonsense. How can you be negatively free from something? It's all just rubbish.'

'It's not like that at all,' says Jen. 'Those are just labels for two different types of freedom. Negative freedom is about being free from external barriers, like being in prison or chained up. Positive freedom is about overcoming your own, internal constraints. It's about being the kind of person you want to be. My teacher says it's a bit like going through a door.'

'A door? What kind of door?'

'Just a door. Any door. A door that has something you want on the other side of it.'

'What kind of thing?'

'Something that's important to you. Something you want in your life. In your case it would probably be the lead singer of Dead or Alive. Negative freedom is about the door being unlocked so you can open it. Positive freedom is about being able to walk through that door and have the thing you want to have.'

'Well I still think it's a load of rubbish,' says Leena.

'Do you? Well maybe if you had a bit more positive freedom yourself you wouldn't see things that way.'

'Oh yeah? Well maybe if you had a bit less negative freedom that wouldn't be such a bad thing either.'

'What do you mean by that?'

'What do you think I mean?'

'I don't know. Why don't you tell me...'

It looks as if I've somehow fallen into the middle of a full-scale cat fight. But then from the far end of the road comes the sound of a motor horn that makes them both look round.

'Hey, that's our ride,' says Jen. 'Gotta go. Nice speaking to you, Adam. See you around.'

The two girls gather up their stuff and rush off towards the yellow minibus waiting at the end of the road. I watch them hasten away; there is definitely some friction between them now. I hope I'm not the cause.

'Adam, where have you been? We went down to Woolworths where you were meant to be but there was no sign of you.'

I have joined Martin and Seagrave at the place we said we would meet. I am about ten minutes late.

'Sorry,' I respond. 'There was nothing going on outside Woolworths so I moved to somewhere else. Down by the harbour. Outside the Mid-Westland Bank.'

Martin had earlier suggested that we all rendezvous at a McDonalds or similar fast food place. However Milford Haven does not have a McDonalds. The closest thing is a Parslows cake shop in one of the shopping arcades. Having got there late I find Martin and Seagrave are already inside, sat at one of the tables. Seagrave is drinking a cup of tea. Martin is drinking a can of Top Deck lemonade shandy. The place is empty apart from us three and a mother with a baby a few tables away.

That baby is making a heck of a lot of noise, crying and grizzling, and the mother is plainly not having a good day.

I sit down, opposite the two of them, on a brown, vinyl banquette that has a multitude of gaffer tape repairs.

'Did you manage to get some responses then?' asks Seagrave.

'Yeah, loads.'

'That's good. It was almost dead where we were. But if you did okay then that's at least something.'

'Yeah, I got plenty,' I tell them. 'There was loads going on down by the harbour.'

I pass my completed worksheet over to Seagrave. He looks it over with an expression that embodies both relief and suspicion. 'You got a lot of responses. These are all genuine, are they?'

'Absolutely,' I tell him,

'You didn't make any of it up?'

'No. I can honestly say that I didn't make up any of that myself.'

'Well you did loads better than us two. Hardly any of the locals wanted to stop and talk to us. Mind you, that was probably more to do with people deliberately avoiding us. On account of Vickers looking like a hooligan and being such a juvenile.'

'Piss off, Seagrave. You didn't do any better than me.'

'That wasn't my fault. I asked plenty of people but they just weren't friendly. None of them wanted to cooperate.'

'Maybe they would have been more helpful if you'd been a bit more approachable.'

'I was approachable.'

'Seagrave, I was there. I saw you talking to them. You were ponsing about like an upper class prick. You're not in sodding Woking. This is Wales. The people who live here are a proud people. They don't like being treated like scum.'

'I resent that, I was respectful to everyone I spoke to...'

A few tables away, that baby is still crying. I've never heard a baby make such a terrible noise. It's wailing away like an air raid siren. The mother is attempting to pacify it but with seemingly little success.

'Besides,' Martin goes on, 'you've seen what this town is like. It's dead. No one is out shopping today. There is nothing going on here. The place could be invaded, a liberating army could literally land on the beach and I still don't think anyone would notice.'

'So what are we going to do then?' Seagrave is starting to look panicky. 'Mr Gardner will do his pieces if we hand in these results. He'll think we have spent the day doing nothing.'

'Relax, will you. It's fine. Look, Gunson has managed to get plenty of results. We can just copy his.'

That baby is continuing to scream and bawl and Seagrave is also looking ill at ease. 'I don't like it,' he says. 'We can't hand in a set of results that look obviously fake.'

'It won't look fake. It'll be okay. Besides, it's only a poxy shopping survey. For Christ's sake man, get a bit of perspective.'

'That's easy for you to say. You may not care about doing this properly, Vickers, but some of us do. Some of us take the work we are doing on this field trip seriously. Some of us want to get good grades for our A Levels. Some of us want to get into a good university.'

'Hey, I want to pass my geography A Level as well, you know. I want the same thing.'

'You do? Really?' Seagrave is almost laughing. 'What, you, Martin Vickers, plan on going to university?'

'Yeah. Well, Southampton Polytechnic. I'm hoping to do social sciences. That's my plan A.'

'Your Plan A?

'Yeah.'

'Doing social science? At Southampton Poly?'

'Yeah.'

'Do you have a Plan B?'

'I do.'

'What's your Plan B?'

'Join the army.'

'My advice is that you focus on Plan B.'

This latest fracas between Martin and Seagrave looks set to continue but they are interrupted again by that screaming baby. Seagrave can take it no more. He turns around and addresses the mother directly: 'Madam, will you please silence that grizzling child. We are A Level students trying to do important work here...'

Chapter 9

'Congratulations, Seagrave. Getting us thrown out of a Parslows cake shop, that's just brilliant.'

'It wasn't my fault. How was I supposed to know she was the manager's sister?'

Following this latest humiliation we make our way back to the car park to await collection. As it happens, the green minibus is already there and waiting for us but, to our surprise, it is not Mr Gardner in the driving seat, it's Mrs Lewis.

Mrs Lewis is a religious studies teacher and is also the Tangley Wood School careers teacher. Thus far in my school journey I have not had very much to do with Mrs Lewis. I didn't choose to do religious studies at either O Level or A Level so I have never had any classes with her. And I have never done anything proactive about any future career so I have avoided her in that context as well. If I had to choose one word to describe Mrs Lewis it would be 'mumsy.' Mrs Lewis is a mumsy-looking woman.

'Hi boys,' she greets us. 'Are Gemma and Rachel not with you?'

'No.'

'Okay. You get in. I just need to pop into the town and get something.' She leaves the minibus unlocked for us and walks briskly off towards the shops. I retrieve my bag from the back of the minibus and shove my shopping survey clipboard into it. In doing so, one of the tapes I've brought with me falls out onto the sand-covered tarmac.

Martin picks it up. 'Hey, what's this? Phil Collins. You don't listen to that crap do you, Gunson?'

I snatch the tape back off him without saying anything.

Seagrave has decided to take this opportunity to eat his lunch. Our packed lunches are provided to us by the hotel kitchen and we've been collecting them each morning after breakfast. Yesterday's offering was a couple of fish paste sandwiches and a tomato, wrapped up for us in grease-proof paper. I extract my lunch from my bag. It appears to be the same as yesterday's. I think about eating it but decide not to.

Mrs Lewis is still not back yet but Gemma Thorneycroft and Rachel Barrett have now returned. They are both carrying a couple of shopping bags. 'Alright boys?' they greet us, grinning. 'Did you manage to get plenty of answers for the survey? We weren't able to get much done ourselves. Would you mind very much if we copied yours...?'

* * *

So Martin doesn't like Phil Collins? The man has no appreciation of good music. It's obvious that we will never be close friends now. I personally think the new album is excellent. I've listened to *No Jacket Required* four times so far on this trip and am liking it more each time I hear it. Maybe it's time for a change though. What other tapes do I have with me?

My friendship with Derek Hotchkiss is almost entirely responsible for what I now know about good music. Prior to receiving guidance from Derek my own record collection consisted of *Abba Greatest Hits Volume 2*, *Parallel Lines* by Blondie and *Superwombling* by The Wombles. I'd never been that much into music until Derek started making tapes for me of stuff that he thought I should be listening to.

Derek did music as an O Level subject and he plays the French horn in the school orchestra. So presumably he knows something about music. His musical tastes are diverse and eclectic, though possibly not as diverse and eclectic as he likes to think they are. The songs he has copied for me include chart music from the likes of Queen and OMD, but also rarities like 'You and I' by Armorica and the twelve inch version of Ultravox's 'One Fine Day'.

One of the first complete albums he taped for me was *Face Value* by Phil Collins. Derek clearly thought a lot of this album as he had gone to the trouble of writing out an inlay card with a track listing and some notes to guide me through it. Any instrumental tracks were annotated with an 'i' to indicate that they were, well, instrumentals and he had put an asterisk alongside those he judged to be 'good tracks'. Scanning the listing revealed that two were instrumental and the remaining nine were all marked as 'good tracks'. I'm sure he meant well, but marking every single song on the album as a 'good track' perhaps offered only limited value for the first time listener.

I pick out another tape from my bag. It's one of Derek's compilations. The tracks on it include songs by Asia, OMD, The Associates, The Lotus Eaters and U2. I slip it into the Walkman, pop on the headphones and allow the music to fill my mind...

Apparently one of the brake lights on the rented, white minibus had stopped working. Mr Gardner, anxious about being stopped by the police, had therefore taken the white minibus to the nearest van rental office (which was in Harverfordwest) to get it looked at. Hence why Mrs Lewis was now driving the green one.

Mr Gardner's intention for the afternoon had been for us to pay a visit to the Green Door of Wales, a sea arch on the southern Pembrokeshire coast. This sea arch, he told us, was as fine an example of a sea arch as any of the ones we had studied in class (e.g. Durdle Door, Dorset). Once the two minibuses had collected us all from Milford Haven, Haverfordwest and Fishguard, the plan was for our reunited group to then drive over there. However the trip turns out to be a total bust. Because the sea arch stands on the edge of army land and today the access to it is closed. So the visit has been abandoned and Martin and I are now back at the hotel, in our room.

'Gardner's a dickhead,' says Martin, 'How could he have been so thick? When the red flag is flying it's a live firing day. Everyone knows that. What a waste of time. We were never going to get access to that sea arch thing. Not if you have to drive through army land to see it.'

'He wasn't at all happy about it,' I add. Mr Gardner is plainly having another bad day. First there was that problem with the white minibus, and now this.

'He should have checked first,' continues Martin, 'before dragging us out all that way for nothing. I'd have been happy just to stay and watch the army manoeuvres from the fence. But he wouldn't let us do that either. None of it surprises me, of course. I always had Gardner down as someone not to be trusted.'

'What makes you say that?'

'He has a beard. The beard is the hallmark of the untrustworthy. My dad taught me that. If a man hides his face behind a beard, what else is he hiding?'

'So you don't trust Mr Gardner because your dad told you not to trust men with beards?'

'Yeah. My dad has given me various bits of valuable advice over the years. Most of it is about who not to trust.'

'Really?' I am moderately intrigued. 'Who else did he say you shouldn't trust?'

'Oh there's all sorts. Bald men, men with long hair, men who wear glasses, men with eyes too close together, men with eyes too far apart, men with no chins, men with thin lips... The list is long.'

While Martin has been speaking Seagrave has entered the room. He slips off his shoes and seats himself cross-legged on the double bed. He settles back against the headboard and brings out a book. At first I'm thinking it's his diary, that thing he was most keen for Martin not to see. But it isn't. It's a school text book.

'What's that you've got there?' asks Martin.

'It's poetry. Part of my A Level English literature syllabus.'

'Poetry? Jesus, Seagrave, you are such a girly swot. We've all got a free afternoon now, thanks to Gardner's cock-up. You should be having fun, enjoying yourself, not reading sodding poetry. Come on, let's go down to the games room.'

'You do what you want,' says Seagrave disdainfully. 'I personally would prefer to keep on top of my other studies.'

I have to admit that, during my time at school, I was of much the same opinion as Martin when it came to poetry. Poetry was not for me. That was something I had established after two years of doing O Level English literature. Which had featured six months of reading

Sohrab and Rustum by Matthew Arnold. Sodding *Sohrab and Rustum*. One of the most tiresome experiences of my whole life

Just in case you don't know the tale of *Sohrab and Rustum*, I'll give you a quick summary. The story takes place hundreds of years ago in the middle of some Russian-sounding place. It tells of how two opposing armies decide to settle the score by way of a single combat, a fight to the death between their two best soldiers. Sohrab is the representative of one army and Rustum the other. But what neither of them knows is that Rustum is Sohrab's father – Rustum had seemingly abandoned the mother without knowing she was having his child. So the two of them engage in this death match without either being aware of the other's identity. As for the ending, let's just say that things don't turn out so well for Sohrab – Rustum is a legendary warrior, older and stronger and far more experienced, so the final result was only ever going to go one way.

What was my beef with *Sohrab and Rustum*, I hear you ask. Well I suppose I had started out with certain expectations of how a poem should be. Expectations that *Sohrab and Rustum* did not live up to. Firstly, it didn't rhyme. Now you might well tell me that poems don't have to rhyme, and that's fair enough. But having a bit of rhyme might at least have made the thing more bearable. Secondly, it was long. I mean, very, very long. Ridiculously long. I had always thought of a poem as something that didn't take up much space. But this one stretched to hundreds of lines. There were pages and pages of the bloody thing. We spent months going through it. It never seemed to end. And thirdly, it was boring. I mean, like, stupifyingly boring. Nothing ever seemed to happen. There was line after line and page after page of literally nothing going on. And once you get to the part where Sohrab is mortally wounded you think that, finally, that's going to be the end, but no, it takes him about ten pages to die.

I failed O Level English literature. My exam grade was unclassified. You might well be thinking that if I had applied myself more and done more revision then I would have passed. But the way I see it, the poems were so incredulously boring and the lessons so mind-numbingly dull that, like Sohrab, I never really stood a chance. No, poems were not for me. Especially poems that had either Sohrab or Rustum in them.

'The poem we're doing at the moment is called *The Rubaiyat of Omar Khayyam*,' says Seagrave. 'I'll read you a bit if you like.'

'I'd rather you didn't,' says Martin. But Seagrave starts reading anyway:

> *'For in and out, above, about, below,*
> *'Tis nothing but a Magic Shadow-show,*
> *Play'd in a Box whose Candle is the Sun,*
> *Round which we Phantom Figures come and go.'*

'What's that then?' asks Martin.

'That's it, that's the poem. Well, one of the verses. There are seventy-five of them. D'you want to hear more?'

'No, you're alright. What's it meant to be about then? Is it about anything?'

'Of course it is.'

'What's it about then?'

'Well it's a metaphor, isn't it? It's saying that the world is like a puppet theatre-type thing and we're all just like puppets being moved around by the forces of destiny.'

Martin, though, has stopped listening. His attention has been drawn to something else. 'Jesus! What's all this on the carpet?'

'What?'

'There's mud all over the carpet. You've done this Seagrave. You've trodden mud all over the carpet just like you did before.'

I move round and take a look. Sure enough, there's mud on the carpet where Seagrave has been walking.

'It wasn't me,' Seagrave pleads.

'Yes it was.' Martin picks up one of Seagrave's docksiders. 'Look, your shoes are covered in it.'

Seagrave must have wandered down on the beach earlier and got some more of that black mud onto his shoes.

'We're all in trouble now thanks to you. Remember that note they left us yesterday?

'Okay, okay,' says Seagrave stroppily. 'We just need to clean it up then, don't we.'

'We? You, you mean. You're the one who caused it.'

'All right, I'll clean it up then. I'll go down to the reception, like the note said, and ask them for the cleaning stuff. Give me back my shoes.'

'No chance, you're not putting those back on. Not with them covered in all that crap. Haven't you got any other shoes?'

'No I haven't.'

'What? How come you've only got one pair of shoes? You brought loads of other rubbish with you.'

'Because I only have one pair of shoes. Okay?' Seagrave crosses his arms petulantly. 'Well I'm not going down there without shoes on. You'll have to go.'

'I'm not doing it. I'm off to the games room. Gunson, you'll have to go.'

'Hey, I'm not doing it,' I respond.

'Well one of us will have to.'

Speaking for myself, I don't really want to go down to the reception desk. I'm conscious of the tricky relationship I now have with the hotel manager. But I can see that this stalemate needs to be broken somehow.

'Okay, look,' I say to Martin. 'I'll go down there as long as you come too. I know it's not ideal but the sooner we get this mess cleared up, the better.'

Martin grudgingly agrees to my offer. We both get ready to leave the room. Seagrave and his shoes, meanwhile, have disappeared into the bathroom, from where a harsh, high-pitched scraping sound can now be heard. As I go to the door I notice that Martin is glancing at the open page of the now discarded poetry book. 'What a load of bollocks. The world is like a magic shadow show? Huh. Muppet show, more like.'

We go downstairs to the hotel reception. No one is present but there is one of those hotel bells on the desk. Martin taps the bell and we wait there together for about ten seconds. Martin then spots Rob Northwood and Paul Armstrong, loafing inside the games room. He disappears off to join them, leaving me alone at the desk. Thanks Martin. The manager appears. It's the same man I had the confrontation with yesterday. This is exactly the situation that I didn't want to put myself in.

'Yes?' the man asks curtly.

'Sorry. Yes. Got a bit of mud on the carpet. In our room,'

Have you ever had that thing where your voice sounds nothing like your voice? When you're facing someone and you're either in trouble or in a stressful situation and your voice sounds totally different to how it usually does. I get that a lot. It happened to me on that earlier occasion with Mr Charlton, the science teacher. It's happening to me again now. 'S-Sorry. If you can let me have the cleaning fluid we'll get it all cleaned up. Thanks.' It must have been my voice because I was the only one talking. But from my side it sounded nothing like it.

The man glares at me, his eyes filled with disgust. That knuckle-shaped face looks like it's going to suddenly spring forward and lay me out flat with a single punch. But instead he disappears out the back and returns carrying a large, plastic bottle and a sponge. 'Here.' He dumps it on the desk in front of me and then disappears again.

'Thanks.' Well, that went about as comfortably as I thought it would. I glance at the printing on the bottle. It describes the contents as 'commercial carpet cleaner' and there are various orange and black warning symbols. It also has some helpful instructions on the label.

'Hey, it's Adam! The pool table guy!' I hear a voice and turn to see that it's Jen. She must have just come in through the front door. Some other Kimble College girls are with her including Leena, her glum-faced associate. 'What're you up to?'

'Oh, hi. I – I came down to get this.'

'Wow, the cleaning fluid. Did you get one of those notes in your room about mud on the carpet? Unlucky. We had one of them too. Don't worry though,' Jen goes on. 'The mud does come out. Eventually.'

'Right. Thanks.'

'Watch out for the fumes, though. And take care not to get it on your fingers. It took your black nail varnish right off, didn't it Leena?'

Leena says nothing, she just rolls her eyes.

'Well, nice seeing you again,' says Jen. 'Have fun with the cleaning fluid.'

Jen smiles at me. The other girls with her also smile, apart from Leena. Leena does not smile. They turn and walk off, giggling as they go. My eyes follow them up the stairs while I remain standing there, cradling my bottle of solvent and feeling like a total dick.

Chapter 10

During my time at Tangley Wood School I had never had many invitations to parties. However that had begun to change once I was in the sixth form. People had started having seventeenth birthday parties, some of them quite elaborate affairs, and I had been invited to a few. Most memorably, back in January Colin Winchester had had a party at his home and I had gone to it. There had been a big turnout for this party, at least thirty people. Derek had gone too and we'd spent most of the time hanging out in the lounge, me drinking supermarket lager and Derek making snide remarks about Colin's record collection.

These parties had many common features and one of them was watching a rented movie. And usually the choice of movie would be a horror film. Now, watching a movie at home in the 1980s was not like it is in the 2020s. It was long before the days of internet downloads and streaming services. If you wanted to see a recent movie at home back then you had to get it on video cassette. And that meant renting a copy from the local corner shop or petrol station.

Colin had had problems renting a movie for the party. This was because his dad, when choosing a video recorder, had decided to go with Betamax. Now, I know there are all kinds of arguments about how the Betamax format was actually superior to the more popular VHS one and I know there are reasons why VHS came to dominate the home video market, but the simple truth was that if you were trying to rent a movie for a Betamax player in the mid-1980s there wasn't a huge amount of choice. However, Colin had eventually managed to find a movie on Betamax that he wanted to watch. The movie was *Galaxy of Terror*.

For those of you who have never seen it, *Galaxy of Terror* is a science fiction horror film where the crew of a spaceship get killed off, one by one, in increasingly gruesome and fantastic ways. I think Colin had chosen this movie because it was the closest thing he could find to a video nasty. If I'm honest, I wasn't that keen on either sci-fi films or horror films. But by the time Colin put the film on I had already imbibed a lot of that supermarket lager so I was content to just sit there on the carpet with everyone else, slumped against the base of the sofa. I didn't really watch the film; I think I just kind of absorbed it.

Like I said, in the movie all of the characters get variously murdered. One of the spaceship's crew is played by the actress who was Joanie Cunningham in *Happy*

Days. She gets killed by having her head ripped apart (a sight that Linda Sterling found especially upsetting). And, perhaps more famously, there's this scene where another female crewmember gets stripped naked and sexually assaulted and killed by this giant alien slug/maggot/centipede thing. I didn't particularly enjoy watching that. I recall thinking that it was all rather disgusting and morally suspect, as did most of the girls in the room. Don't get me wrong – I was a sixteen-year-old boy, brimming with interest in the opposite sex. But no, even at that age I felt that any video of a woman being molested by a massive maggot was not a healthy thing to be watching. I do remember it well though because a) Colin insisted on rewinding and replaying the scene seven times and b) this was literally the most sex I had ever seen on a television.

You have to remember that in the 1980s there was no internet, no world wide web, no free and easy online access to vast reams of sexual content. Pornography was much harder to come by. I certainly had seen very little of it. Occasionally you'd get the likes of Paul Armstrong standing outside the school gate with a copy of a top shelf magazine. And there was that one time when an extract from *Razzle* was being passed around the back of a maths class. But that was pretty much it. And that scene in *Galaxy of Terror*, revolting as it was, would remain the most sex I had yet seen on a TV. Until, that was, the Wednesday night of the field trip.

* * *

It was during dinner that evening that Chas Browning told us all what he had learnt. 'The hotel has a film service. Adult films. Broadcast on the TVs in the rooms at eight o'clock every night. One of the guys from the other school told me. To watch it you need to tune the TV in your room to channel nine. If you ask at the reception desk they'll tell you what they're showing. Tonight it's *The Wicked Lady*.'

Martin Vickers was all over this as soon as he heard about it. He is determined that we are going to watch this film tonight. Stuart Seagrave of course disagrees. He wants to watch an episode of *Star Trek* on BBC2 that happens to overlap with the start of the film.

'Bollocks to that,' says Martin. 'We're watching the film. We're not watching some crappy episode of *Star Trek*. What do you want to watch that for, anyway? It's just a repeat. *The Wicked Lady* is a new film.'

'I thought *The Wicked Lady* was an old film,' says Seagrave. 'Black and white. Made in the 1940s. I remember watching it. Wasn't it on BBC1 on Sunday afternoon a few weeks back?'

'This is a remake. A new version. It's got Faye Dunaway in it. And John Gielgud. Proper actors. Proper Hollywood stars. Gunson, you want to see it, don't you? Of course he does. And so do I. So that's decided then.'

Seagrave reluctantly agrees, but only so long as we can watch the first half of *Star Trek* before the film starts. The *Star Trek* episode is one I remember seeing before. It's the one where a transporter accident causes

Captain Kirk to be split into two separate versions of himself. We can't get too into it though because, once eight o'clock comes round, Martin gets up and switches over to channel nine. As Chas had predicted, *The Wicked Lady* starts showing on the screen. And the first thing we see is a scene of a seventeenth century English village with a naked girl running down the street.

'What the hell!' exclaims Seagrave. 'We can't watch this.'

'What's the matter with you now?'

'It's a porn film. I'm not watching a porn film.'

'It isn't a porn film. It's a proper movie. There, look at that.' Martin points at the credits now showing on the screen in front of the naked girl. 'See? Directed by Michael Winner. The guy who did the *Death Wish* movies. That's a sign of quality.'

'What if Mr Gardner comes in and catches us watching this?'

'He won't come in. He's probably watching it himself. Just sit quietly and watch the film, for God's sake.'

We each settle down to watch the movie, me in the lower bunk bed, Seagrave on the double bed and Martin in the chair next to the door. Seagrave was probably thinking that this new *Wicked Lady* film was going to more or less be a remake of the 1940s version. But, whilst largely following the same plot, it is clear from the start that this is no Sunday afternoon movie. I don't think you could really call it a porn film but it does contain a lot of sex and a lot of nudity.

There's this one, lengthy scene that shows a naked couple getting down to it on a fireside carpet. And there's another where Faye Dunaway and this other woman start going at each other with whips. During this fight with whips the other woman's dress is rapidly ripped and torn off her and she is forced to continue fighting topless. Faye Dunaway's outfit though remains strangely intact throughout. In fact, Faye Dunaway manages to keep most of her clothes on for the duration of the film, which I'm guessing was a contractual thing.

'What did you think of that then, Seagrave?' asks Martin when the film is over.

'I thought it was rubbish,' says Seagrave dismissively. 'Filth and a load of rubbish.'

'Why? What's the matter with you? Did you have a problem looking at a few naked girls? I didn't hear you complaining. I didn't see you hiding you head under the blanket. Well I enjoyed it and so did Gunson. I thought it was quite educational, actually.'

'Educational?'

'Yeah. A nice bit of history.'

'A nice bit of history? Vickers, there was absolutely no historical accuracy in that film.'

'Really? So what do you know about it then?'

'I know that women in the seventeenth century didn't wear underwear like *that*.'

'Oh, right. So you're an expert on that, are you? Why am I not surprised? Are you seriously trying to tell me that you didn't like any of it?'

'Well,' says Seagrave after a few moments thinking, 'I suppose the music was all right.'

'The music? Really? You thought the music was the best thing about the film?' Martin turns away in disbelief. 'Unbelievable. Well I thought it was a good movie and so did Gunson. So I'm sorry, Seagrave, that you had to miss the end of Captain Kirk and watch a movie full of naked girls instead. But I'll tell you one thing: you'll never see women like that in any crappy sci-fi show like *Star Trek*.'

Seagrave and Martin continue to bicker as they have done ever since they first unpacked their bags. And so the evening comes to an end and the lights go out and I'm left lying in my bunk bed, reflecting on the events of another crazy day.

We must have spent hours scrubbing that carpet, Seagrave and I. Martin was of course absent – he didn't come back to the room until hours later. I can still smell the solvent now, despite having left the windows open all evening. It can't be good for you, breathing in those fumes. And when, after we'd finished, I returned the cleaning stuff back to reception, I got the same silent, contemptuous response from the hotel manager as I had before.

We had got the writing up of the survey results done as well. Mr Gardner had looked in on us after dinner. He seemed to be happy enough with the completed work we showed him, although he did comment that the responses from the shoppers of Milford Haven appeared to be a little unusual.

I'm thinking about Jen. What she had said to me earlier. She told me I was fearless. She plainly doesn't know me very well. She also said I don't talk much. What was that about? I suppose it might be true. Other people have told me the same thing in the past – about me being a quiet person, not much of a talker. I've never felt like I'm a quiet person myself, though. It always seems like there's so much stuff going on inside my head, so much noise, so many thoughts buzzing around. The inside of my head never feels like a quiet place. And, in the conversations that go on inside my head, I'm the one doing most of the talking.

Jen had said she was studying politics and philosophy. I don't remember everything she had said about it. There was certainly something about her, though. Something about the way her face lit up while she was telling me all that philosophy stuff. Something that I couldn't help being drawn to.

Politics doesn't interest me at all. The closest I have ever come to engaging in politics was when the upper sixth form had staged a mock general election back in February. It had all been taken very seriously at the time, as I recall. There were candidates selected from the upper sixth form students, one standing as Conservative, one for Labour and others for the Liberals and the Social Democrats. Stuart Seagrave had tried to ally himself with the Conservative faction but they had turned him away; apparently not even the Tories wanted Seagrave.

It had all been very intense, with manifestos presented and debates organised and that sort of thing. All the effort had been a total waste of time, though. The election had been won by Cathy Remington, a smart-looking upper sixth girl whose life plan was to have a career as a catwalk model. Cathy didn't represent any party and she didn't have any policies. In fact, her campaign tag-line was, 'Sod the policies, just vote for me.' She had won by a landslide.

Jen had said that her name wasn't short for Jennifer and it wasn't short for Jenny either. But it must be short for something. Surely she couldn't just be called Jen. What about Jenna? Is Jenna a name? There was a sci-fi show on TV a while back that had a character called Jenna. Maybe Jen is short for Jenna.

What was that thing that Jen and Leena had been arguing about? Positive and negative freedom – yes, that was it. I think I tend to agree with Leena's views on that one. How can you be negatively free from something? It just sounds ridiculous. Derek has this notion he uses to check whether an idea is worthy of his time. He calls it the 'stupid' test. Does negative freedom pass the 'stupid' test? I don't think it does.

But Jen had also mentioned positive freedom. What did she say positive freedom was? Having the ability to be the kind of person you want to be. Being able to go through the doors you want to go through. That sounds a lot more attractive, that's something I could get excited about. I wonder if my own life is lacking in positive freedom. Maybe it is. Maybe if I possessed a bit more positive freedom I would have already asked Roz Madsen to go out with me by now?

And then it occurs to me that this is the first time in almost two days that I have thought about Roz.

Chapter 11

It's not good, being stuck in the house all day, never going out, never seeing or talking to anybody. Lockdown is a total nightmare. Zoom calls are all well and good but there's no substitute for having a person physically in front of you. It's been ages since I last saw anyone face to face. It's also been weeks since I last had someone come to my front door. Things are definitely getting to me. Whenever I used to get someone knocking on my door I always resented the interruption, but now there's no one knocking on my door I almost miss it.

Who was the last human soul that I physically met face to face? Oh yes, it was that Liberal candidate campaigning for the (subsequently postponed) town council elections. A stout, grey-haired man with big glasses and a suit that he'd probably been wearing for the past fifteen years.

'Are there any concerns you have about the local area?' he had asked me.

'Well,' I had answered after a moment's consideration, 'what about all the pot holes? The roads around here are in a shocking condition.'

'That's not my responsibility. Roads are dealt with by the county council.'

'You're telling me the roads aren't your responsibility?'

'No. I'm on the town council. Roads are county council.'

'So you're not going to do anything about the roads?'

'Not my responsibility.'

'I see,' I had replied. 'Well maybe you need to *take* some responsibility. Maybe if you *took* some responsibility for problems instead of kicking the can down the road then maybe people might think about voting for you, maybe.'

He had thanked me for my time and moved onto the house next door.

Philosophy. I don't know, maybe all it *is* good for is teaching you how to win an argument...

The third morning of the field trip is another bright, warm morning. Today we're doing hydrology. Examining a quiet stretch of the River Solva, about fifteen miles north of Shore Haven. Our task is to work out the discharge of the river at various places along its course. To do this you need to know the width and depth of the river at different points and the speed at which the water is flowing. We are still working in the same groups and are spread out along the river. Stuart Seagrave is currently wearing blue swimming trunks and is stood, thigh-deep, in the middle of the stream. He is clutching a flow meter – a length of tube with a propeller-type device on one end that we are to use to measure the speed of the water (Mr Gardner had warned us that these flow meters were precision instruments and were to be handled with care and delicacy). Seagrave is calling out a bunch of numbers that we are supposed to be writing down.

'Thirty-two, then thirty-eight, and then after that forty-one. Hey, are either of you two getting this down?' Seagrave is not happy. I think he would have preferred to have been in more of a command position, stood on the bank whilst Martin Vickers and I were the ones out in the water. But instead it is he who is doing all the wet work.

'Got it,' I call back to him, noting down that latest set of figures on my clipboard. I'm stood at the side of the river. Martin is sat down on the grass behind me. As usual, Martin is not making much contribution to the field work. Instead he is currently gazing downstream to the spot, about twenty yards away, where Gemma Thorneycroft and Rachel Barrett are supposedly doing their own river measurements. Both Gemma and Rachel have stripped off and are wearing red bikinis. They have not spent much time in the water; instead they have for most of the morning been lying on the bank in a recumbent position, soaking up the sun.

'You do both realise that this water is absolutely freezing.'

'Just get on with it, Seagrave,' says Martin. 'The sooner you get it all done and finished, the sooner you can get out.'

'I'm surprised you weren't keen to go in the river yourself.'

'Yeah...' says Martin. '...well, I forgot my swimming trunks. It was just unlucky that I didn't bring them.'

'That was very convenient, wasn't it,' says Seagrave indignantly, 'especially seeing as how we were specifically told to bring swimming trunks in our last geography lesson. I'm just a bit surprised that you weren't up for it. I would have thought that wading out into a fast-flowing river was just the kind of thing an SAS commando would want to be involved with.'

'Like I said, I forgot my trunks. Besides, the SAS is the Special Air Service. They don't do rivers.'

I have to confess that I forgot to pack swimming trunks as well. Part of me is relieved that, with my feet still covered in those blisters from Tuesday, I don't have to go wading out into that riverbed. I do feel a little bit of guilt, though, that Seagrave has been forced into it. Not a lot of guilt, just a little.

This is actually not the first time I have done a river study like this. Back when I was doing O Levels we did a very similar thing on a local stream in Woking. Well, I say stream, but it was really more of a drain, full of debris and litter. What made that day stand out was the location – the stream was right next to the fence that enclosed the local rival school. And the time we were doing this stream study happened to coincide with the lunchbreak. So there was my O Level geography class trying to do this work while the whole time there were kids from the rival school lined up on the other side of the fence, shouting abuse and throwing dirt and generally subjecting us to ridicule. Thankfully, on that earlier occasion the stream was so shallow that none of us had had to put on swimming trunks in order to measure it.

Once all the river measuring is done Seagrave wades back to the riverbank. 'Here, can one of you take this?'

He hands the flow meter to Martin, who tosses it down on the bank next to where we left our bags.

'You are unbelievable, Vickers,' Seagrave moans while drying off his white, spindly legs with a towel. 'We are supposed to be measuring the river, not staring at Gemma and Rachel in their swimwear. Anyway, I thought you said you didn't fancy any of the girls that go to our school.'

'I don't. I wouldn't go out with any girl who goes to Tangley Wood.'

'Yes, well, I'm very sorry that, of the seventy girls in our year group, none of them manage to meet the required Martin Vickers standard. Have you ever considered that, perhaps, you are a bit too picky?'

Martin thinks about this for a moment. 'There's nothing wrong with being selective,' he says. 'Actually, some of the girls in that other school staying at the hotel look quite nice. Did you see them this morning when we were having breakfast?'

'Yes, I did.' Seagrave is intrigued. 'Which one of them do you fancy then? The pale one with the black hair?'

'What, the bony one? The one who looks like she sleeps in a coffin? God no, I don't fancy her. Her friend looks quite nice though. The one with the ponytail. She looks alright.'

'Is that so?' says Seagrave. 'And what is it that you like about her? Is it, by any remote chance, because you think she's got nice tits?'

Are they talking about Jen? It sounds like they're talking about Jen. I don't like this. I don't like it at all. But Martin doesn't get a chance to answer as we suddenly hear Mr Gardner's voice calling us; our time here is done and we need to pack up our things.

With the measuring of the River Solva now complete (and Seagrave now reunited with his trousers) we rendezvous back at the minibuses. Mr Gardner is apparently feeling the heat this morning – he has removed his jumper to reveal a Yes tee-shirt that he has on underneath. A couple of the girls ask him about it. The tee-shirt is a memento of the band's 1977 'Close to the Edge' tour. He tells them that he has been a Yes fan since the early seventies. If Mr Gardner is into prog rock bands like Yes then maybe he has a mellow side that I haven't seen yet.

Derek tried to get me into prog rock, stuff like King Crimson and Genesis and Yes. Music from his mum's record collection. I was okay with Genesis, because of the Phil Collins connection, but I drew the line at Yes. I do not like the music of Yes. I do not like it at all. I had to tell Derek quite forcibly; please do not give me recordings of any more music by Yes.

Mr Gardner's plan for the afternoon is for us to go and see the Llys-y-fran reservoir and dam. However once we are all together a problem becomes apparent – Chas Browning has got a bit too adventurous and has managed to cut his arm on some barbed wire. He needs a tetanus jab, which means driving back to Shore Haven and finding a doctor. Hence, a short time later we find ourselves back in the hotel car park. Mr Gardner is, of course, irritated by this latest disruption to his finely-planned itinerary. Mrs Lewis, though, is more sympathetic and says that it's the kind of accident that could have happened to anyone.

After checking with the hotel reception it turns out that there is no doctor's surgery in Shore Haven. The closest is in Broad Haven, a couple of miles down the coast. The teachers tell us there will be about an hour's delay while they drive Chas there and get him sorted. We are all to meet back here at twelve and be ready to move.

Seagrave has been wearing his wet swimming trunks underneath his trousers since leaving the river so he takes the opportunity to go back to the room and get changed. Martin wanders off round the back of the car park with Rob Northwood and Paul Armstrong. The rest of the group disperse variously either into the hotel or up the road towards the shops.

I'm wondering what to do with myself. I don't really fancy going back up to the room with Seagrave. Isaac is kicking his heels around the hotel entrance – I don't think I can handle any more of Isaac's monotone voice droning on about alien contact and how the universe is made up of wheels within wheels. Then I remember that I still need to get a postcard to send to my mum and dad. Relieved to have a legitimate excuse to get out of there, I head off up the road towards the post office.

The post office has a few different postcards to choose from, displayed in one of those revolving stands out on the pavement. I select one that has a photo of the Shore Haven sea stacks and go inside to pay. Inside there's a small queue for the till that includes, just ahead of me, Linda and Julie who are buying sweets. And also there, browsing the shelves of the small supermarket area, is Jen. I feel my heart leap upon seeing her.

'Hello you!' she says, seeing me approach. 'What are you doing here?'

'Just getting a postcard. To send to my mum and dad.'

'Nice.'

'We're only here a couple more days so I need to get it posted, you know, before we leave.'

'Yeah,' says Jen. 'Our lot leaves tomorrow morning. Tonight is our last night here. I was hoping this place would have my favourite biscuits. There aren't many shops that sell them. Leena ate all the ones I had left. She said it wasn't her but I know full well it was. Honestly, sharing a room with that girl is such a nightmare. And she has a real mean streak as well. Always saying cruel things about people. Lord knows what she says about me behind my back. I hate people who are like that. Don't you?'

'Yeah,' I nod in reply, 'people like that are really... chronic.'

Linda and Julie slide past me, having just purchased a tube of Refreshers and a Yorkie bar. They glance at me and Jen together and I can hear them giggling as soon as they are on the other side of the door. Are they going to tell everyone else that they'd spotted me chatting with this girl? Surprisingly, I discover that I don't care.

'What have you been up to this morning?' Jen asks.

'Hydrology. Measuring the discharge of a river.'

'Uhuh. We did that on Tuesday. Today we've been doing coastal drift. Down on the beach.'

I get to my turn at the till. The woman serving asks me if I want a stamp as well as the postcard. I tell her I do. Jen asks if they have any Choco Leibniz biscuits. The woman says they don't and suggests chocolate hobnobs as an alternative. Jen thanks her but declines. I pay for the card and stamp.

'Yeah. that was a really boring morning,' says Jen as we both leave. 'Two hours looking at pebbles.'

I nod along in agreement and start sharing my own pebble-measuring highlights. Then I remember I still have that stone in my pocket, the one with the writing on. 'I found this on the beach on Tuesday ,' I say, handing it to her.

Jen examines the letters on the stone, her eyes showing the same flashes of intensity that I saw in them when she was playing Space Invaders. 'It says "Principal Parts".'

'Yeah.'

'What does that mean? Principal parts of what?'

'No idea. None of us can work it out.'

'Hmm, well it must have meant something important to someone.'

Walking along the street next to Jen is a thrilling experience. Instead of her college jumper she is wearing a green and white, Breton-style top. She looks supercool. I wish Derek had let me borrow his black Levi jacket. I would be looking so much smoother wearing that, instead of this poxy anorak. The weight of that stone from the beach has now torn a hole in one of the pockets. That's just great. A coat that's got a hole in a pocket, when's that ever going to be a good thing to have?

I recall Jen telling me how I didn't talk much. I can't be having that. I need to think of something else to say to her.

'So,' I begin, hesitantly, 'your name is Jen?'

'It is.'

'But Jen isn't short for Jennifer or Jenny?'

'Correct Jenny's not my name. Neither is Jennifer.'

'Is it Jenna?'

'No it's not Jenna.'

'What is it then?'

'Like I said, you can call me Jen.'

We walk on a bit further.

'Okay then Adam,' she says. 'Tell me, what are your plans?'

'My plans?'

'For the future. You must have some plans for the future. What are you going to do when you finish college?'

'Dunno. I guess I'll just get a job or something. An office job. In a bank or an insurance company. Something like that.'

'Well that doesn't sound very exciting. Not the kind of life I pictured for an intrepid guy like you. Do you not want to go to university?'

'No.'

'Really? Are you sure?'

'Yes. Actually, I was thinking about having a go at writing.'

'Writing?' I can see Jen's face light up again. 'Writing what?'

'A novel.'

'A novel about what?'

'Oh, I don't know yet. I haven't given it much thought.'

'Hmm. What A Level subjects are you doing?'

'Geography, chemistry and maths.'

'And what made you choose those?'

'They were the ones I had the best predicted O Level results for.'

'I see...' She considers my answer. 'Well I'm not so sure those subjects will be of much use to you. Not if you want to be a writer. No, if you want to be a writer you need to have some experiences. You need to have something to write about. My advice is to go and get yourself some experiences. Find an adventure somewhere. Hey, have you seen this place?'

We've wandered the whole length of the street now and are back outside the hotel. Jen is gazing at the derelict building on the other side of the road, the place called the Cocktail Club.

'What do you suppose this is?'

'Some kind of abandoned bar, I'm guessing.'

'Yeah. Come on, let's check it out.'

There's a door on the side closest to us. She goes up to it and tries it. 'Hmm, I don't think it's locked but it doesn't want to open. Here, you have a go.'

'Are you sure? It doesn't look very safe. And there are signs. They don't seem to want people going in there.'

The hotel manager already views me as a reprobate for multiple reasons. I'm not keen to add breaking and entering to my growing list of crimes.

'Oh come on,' says Jen. 'You're the fearless guy who breaks into pool tables and stares people down, Busting into this place should be easy. If you're gonna be a writer you need to be curious about things. Come on, I said you needed an adventure and there's one right here, waiting for you.'

Okay, I admit it; it's hard to say no to her when she smiles at me like that. I try pushing the door. It looks like it should open inwards but it's old and warped – reluctant to give up its secrets. I give it a couple of shoves with my shoulder and, on the second go, it stiffly jerks open, pushing out a cloud of sand and dust.

We both step in through the open door. The place has obviously been abandoned for some time. The only light coming in is through the small cracks in the roof. In the gloom it's hard to tell what the place had been in its former life. There are a bunch of dusty, rotting cardboard boxes stacked up inside. Visible evidence suggests that the most recent inhabitants have been seagulls, and I can glimpse a dead seagull (or rather half a dead seagull) in the far corner.

I'm not sure it's a good idea to hang around in here but Jen seems to be loving it. 'Wow, look at this place,' she says. 'This is amazing. It must have been some kind of bar to serve customers out on the beach. Not exactly Club Tropicana now though, is it? I wonder if there's still any drink in here.'

I'm sincerely hoping that she doesn't find any. I like being with Jen but she is beginning to show a bit of a reckless streak. She starts rootling around underneath the bar area, disturbing several dead spiders in the process. She doesn't find any alcohol and, to be honest, I'm not disappointed.

'Come on, let's try opening up these shutters.' Both shutters are padlocked down but the wood around the latches is so rotten that she has no problem releasing them. The shutters roll up, emitting more dust and spiders in the process. What is revealed is a fine, panoramic view of the beach and the sea.

'Wow, how good is this?' says Jen. 'What a great place. I wonder why they closed it?'

I treat this as a rhetorical question but suspect that the notice outside saying 'building condemned' may have had some bearing on things.

'Imagine having a job working in a bar like this,' she says. 'That would be so cool.'

'Is that a job you would do then?' I ask.

'Probably not long-term,' says Jen. 'But as an evening job while at university, this would be great. Of course I need to get myself to university first. I'm hoping to get into Bath. Bath University. They have a good philosophy course at Bath. Assuming I can get the right A Level grades to get in, that is. Sorry, I hope I'm not being boring. Leena says that I talk too much about philosophy, that I become really boring when I start telling other people about it. Not that Leena knows anything about anything, of course, but I know I do go on about it a lot. I'm not boring you, am I?'

'No.' I try to assure her.

'I just have this passion for it. There are so many things that I'm curious about. So much that I want to understand. Like the mind, for example. Consciousness.

The thing that makes you *you* and me *me*. What is it? Where does it come from? Do you ever wonder about that, Adam?'

'You mean, do I wonder why we are here? Where we came from? Well... yes, I guess so.'

'The thing is,' Jen continues, 'you have the brain which is the physical thing inside your head. And then you have the mind. The stuff that happens inside the brain. Thinking. Consciousness. The soul, if you want to call it that. What I want to know is, where does the mind bit come from? Is it just caused by the workings of the brain? Is it just the result of electrochemical stuff happening inside the brain? Or does it come from somewhere else? Is it put inside us when we are born, by God or whatever? And what happens when we die? Do our minds just disappear into nothing? Like when you switch off a micro-computer and the program you typed in just disappears. Is it like that when we die? Or do our minds go off somewhere else? Do they carry on existing somewhere else somehow, in some form or other?'

'You mean like a spirit or a ghost or something?'

'Yeah. It's something I've always wondered about. I'm hoping that studying philosophy will help me find the answer. I've recently started reading about Descartes. René Descartes. You heard of him?'

I tell her that I haven't. I know there's a René in the TV show *'Allo 'Allo!* but I'm guessing it isn't the same guy.

'Descartes is reckoned to be the father of modern philosophy. Although he does have some questionable views about animal welfare. But, setting that aside, he had this big idea about the mind and the body being separate things. Cartesian Dualism, it's known as. Descartes reckoned that our bodies are made of physical matter and our minds are made of some other stuff. And when your body dies your mind is able to separate from the body and continue existing, well, separately. So if that's right it would mean that our minds might somehow be able to carry on living after death. If Descartes was right then the problem we have to find the answer to is, if the mind *is* made of something other than physical matter, then what is it made of? And how can the body, which *is* made of physical matter, be connected to something that isn't? You see the problem, yes?'

I nod along, making appropriate 'mmm' sounds and trying to look like I understand what she's talking about.

'Of course, Descartes lived hundreds of years ago. Back then the world was a much simpler place. People thought that everything was made out of just four elements, earth, air, fire and water. And everything was supposedly made up out of different combinations of those four elements. Something I recently learnt was that ancient people had their own theory of gravity. We all think that Isaac Newton was the first person to notice stuff falling down, but ancient people had their own ideas about it. They thought earth and water fell downwards because it was in the nature of those two elements to fall down, to return to where they came from. And similarly it was in the nature of air and fire to rise up. And because the sky and the stars didn't go up or down they thought that the heavens must be made of something else. Something other than the four elements. So they came up with a fifth element and said that the heavens were made out of that. They called it quintessence. Quintessence literally means the fifth element. Did you know that? And there were some people who started thinking, maybe our minds are made out of this quintessence? Maybe God makes our minds from quintessence and puts them in our bodies when we are born. And then when we die our minds leave our bodies and go back up to heaven because it's in the nature of things made from quintessence to return to where they came from.'

I don't think I have ever heard anyone say the word 'quintessence' as many times as Jen has. We gaze out at the waves rolling forward onto the beach. On the far horizon is an oil tanker, a vague, fuzzy shape making its way slowly north across the base of the sky.

'But of course,' Jen continues, 'we now know that our bodies are not just made out of four elements. We're made of atoms and protons and electrons and sub atomic particles. But maybe there is something else. Something we don't yet know about. Something like quintessence. Something that our minds are made of.'

'Yes. Right.' I'm trying to look like I'm totally on top of what she's talking about. A seagull flaps by, close to the window. It looks for an instant as if it might want to return to its roost inside the Cocktail Club, but it just flies past, squawking.

'And of course,' says Jen, 'there are loads of other things I'm curious about as well. For instance, do we have free will or is that just an illusion? Are we all really just following along some pre-determined path laid out by God or whatever?'

'What, you mean like puppets in a puppet show?'

'Yes, precisely. Or are we just like characters in a book and the storyteller is the one who decides our ultimate fate? Who knows? Hey, maybe even the storyteller themselves is just a creation of someone else. How messed up would that be! And another possibility is that we're all just dreaming and everything that we think of as being real isn't actually real at all, it's all just a dream. We like to think we know what is real and what isn't, but who knows what kind of unknown complexities there might be? There could be layer upon layer upon unknown layer for all we know.'

'You mean like wheels within wheels?'

'Yeah, exactly that. Wheels within wheels.' She looks at me, smiling. 'So what do you think, Adam? Do you think our whole lives are just a dream? Or do you think that everything that happens to us is just pure chance, just random stuff? Or do you think that there is some higher force of destiny that has brought the two of us here together at this precise moment in time?'

And then Jen leans across and kisses me.

Chapter 12

During the months that I had been obsessing over Roz I had discussed various options with Derek. Various possible ways of creating a situation that would enable me to ask her out. One of these involved badminton club. Badminton club was held in the school sports hall every Wednesday after school. I had it on good authority that Roz went to badminton club and I thought that it might give me a good opportunity to both find a time to ask her out and also to see her wearing her gym skirt. Derek wasn't keen though. He had no interest in playing badminton and, as there was no way I was going on my own, that didn't happen.

Instead, Derek suggested I come along to the school orchestra rehearsals. Roz was in the orchestra and played the piccolo. Derek was also in the orchestra and played the French horn. He had said it would be even better if I played an instrument myself, such as the trombone (there was always a shortage of trombonists, apparently), as that would give me a more straightforward 'in', so to speak. But learning the trombone was not something I would be able to do quickly so, instead, Derek told me to come along as an observer,

Rehearsals took place in the school music room on Tuesday lunchtimes. The orchestra members all sat in a semicircle with their instruments while Mr Thompson, the music teacher, stood at the front, conducting. Derek, very conveniently, had a seat at the end of the brass section so it was easy for me to grab a chair and sit alongside him. This spot also gave me a good view of Roz where she sat, among the other girls playing oboes, clarinets, piccolos and flutes. I was concerned that Mr Thompson might ask me what the hell I thought I was doing sitting there but he didn't seem to care or be interested.

I waited and observed as the orchestra started setting up. The sheet music for the session was passed around. Derek took the music for his instrument and arranged it on the stand in front of him, with the sheet for the first piece they were going to practice at the front. It had 'tacet' written at the top of it. The rest of the sheet was just blank staves.

'What's that?' I asked.

'That's my sheet of music for this piece.'

'But there's no music on it.'

'That's right. There's no music for the French horn in this piece.'

'No music? And they still give you a sheet of music, even though there's no music on it?'

'Yes.'

My first thought was that this was plain ridiculous. What was the point of being in an orchestra with an instrument that doesn't play anything? Surely this did not pass the 'stupid' test. But then my second thought was, hey, what an opportunity. If playing the French horn meant simply sitting there and not doing anything then that was something I could do myself. I wondered if there was anywhere I might obtain a spare French horn. Then I would have a genuine, legitimate reason for being there, rather than sitting on the end of the row and probably looking a bit suspect.

Of course the main reason for me being there was Roz. I sat there throughout the rest of the practice session watching her play her piccolo. I don't think there was much music for the piccolo in that piece either as she spent more time not playing her piccolo than she did playing it. But when she was playing it and she had her lips wrapped around the mouthpiece I found myself wondering how long it would be before her lips were wrapped around my own lips instead of that piccolo. The point I am trying to get to here is that I had never kissed a girl before and I was as confident as anything that Roz Madsen would be the first girl that I would kiss.

And then Jen leans across and kisses me. I mean, she properly kisses me. Her lips touch mine and she hesitates slightly at first and then she puts her hand round the back of my head and pulls my face towards her and kisses me.

Then she pulls back and her brown eyes gaze into mine. 'Well,' she says, 'I think we can scratch off the possibility of everything being just a dream.' She glances around the dank, dusty interior we are stood in. 'Hmm. It probably isn't a great idea to spend too long in this place, is it? Not with all this dirt and stuff. I have to be going now anyway. We've got another fun activity this afternoon. Analysing glacial deposits, which will probably be just as boring as it sounds. But meet me later, yes? In the games room? About four o'clock?'

And the next moment she's gone, swiftly out the door, and I'm stood there on my own with my clothes covered in dust and sand and my heart all over the place, frankly.

Wow! Did you see that coming? I certainly didn't. That was incredible! I've just been kissed by a girl for the first time ever and, in all truth, I think it was probably the quintessence of what a first kiss should be. And I have a date with her. Well, a sort of date. At four o'clock today. Again, wow!

I check my watch. It's time I was getting back to the minibus so I need to get moving. I try pulling the shutters back down. They come down okay but the lock mechanism is broken. The door also won't close properly but I do the best I can with it.

Has anyone seen me? I don't think so. I cross over the road, brushing the sand and dust and dead spiders off my clothes as I go. I walk round the side of the hotel towards the car park. And suddenly I'm face to face with Mrs Lewis.

'Adam Gunson, what are you doing?'

'Me, Miss? Nothing, Miss.'

Did she see us just now? Did she see me and Jen together?

'Where have you been? You're late. We're ready to get going.'

'I've just been down to the post office, Miss.' I show her my postcard.

'Do you know where Isaac is?'

'Isaac? No, Miss, I haven't seen him.'

'Okay, go and get yourself on the minibus.'

Mrs Lewis continues round to the front of the hotel. She couldn't have seen me and Jen together. If she had she would surely have said something. I head on over to where the two minibuses are parked and climb into the green one. I am greeted with a cheer from the other occupants. Did any of them see me with Jen? Or are they cheering because I'm the last one here? I smile an apologetic grin back at them all and sit down next to Chas Browning. Chas is going on about how unexpectedly painful his tetanus injection was. I carry on smiling. I can't stop smiling at the moment.

I wish Derek was here, so I could tell him all about what has just happened to me. I really want to tell someone about it. Is there anyone in the minibus that I could tell?

On the seats in front are Julie Whitworth and Linda Sterling. Could I tell them? I don't think so. How about Colin and Chas? No, probably not. And behind me are Martin Vickers and Stuart Seagrave. Absolutely not.

Through the window I see Mrs Lewis walking back into the car park. Accompanying her are Mr Gardner and Isaac. Whatever crazy stuff Isaac was getting up to, he has now been found. He and Mrs Lewis head over to the white minibus while Mr Gardner climbs into the driver's seat of the green one.

'Right, hush up you lot.' Mr Gardner turns his head and addresses us as he starts the engine. 'We're already late and I don't want any more messing about from any of you.'

The minibuses drive off out of the car park, once again in convoy.

Robotically, I reach around in my bag to fetch the Walkman and a tape to listen to. I find my copy of *The Hits Album*. I'd forgotten that I'd brought that. Well, I say *The Hits Album*, but of course what I had was the cassette version which was called *The Hits Tape* (a two tape set). It was another of the few records that I'd actually gone out and bought myself, rather than a copy Derek had made for me.

Derek thought that I'd made a bad choice with this one, as in his view the *Now That's What I Call Music* compilations were superior. But I quite like *The Hits Album*. The songs on it are grouped into sections – side one is pop songs, side two, soul; side three, ballads; side four, rock – so you can pick out your preferred music genre.

However, in spite of it being called *The Hits Album*, there are quite a number of tracks on it that were not, to my certain knowledge, hits. Also, it has a cut-down version of Michael Jackson's 'Thriller' that is missing its final section, the part where Vincent Price does his 'Edgar Alan Poe' bit. Which is very annoying because, let's be honest, that bit is everyone's favourite bit.

I still like *The Hits Album* though. *The Hits Album* is cool. But I don't want to listen to *The Hits Album*. In fact I don't want to listen to any music right now. The minibus heads north towards the Llys-y-fran reservoir. I put the Walkman and the tape back in my bag and I just gaze out of the window at the passing fields.

Jen is amazing. I've never met anyone like her. I can't wait to see her again. The way she smiled at me when she was leaving. I've never had anyone smile at me like that before. It was incredible.

I wish I had had more to say when we were together just now. She's called me out once already for not being much of a talker. I need to have something ready to talk to her about when I meet her at four o'clock. I don't want her getting the impression that I'm some sort of waster with no drive or ambition.

Hmm, what do I know about that would be a good topic of conversation? Years of making Airfix models and reading *Battle Action* comic has left me with the ability to name all the different types of weapon used in

World War Two. Is that knowledge going to prove helpful? Probably not. How about music? I wonder what kind of music she likes. Does she like Phil Collins? I hope she's not into heavy metal. I don't like heavy metal.

It would be even better, of course, if I had something intelligent to say about that philosophy stuff that she is so into. I wish I knew more about it. What was that poem Seagrave had been reading yesterday? Something about the world being like a puppet shadow show. That sounds a bit like philosophy. Maybe I could borrow that off Seagrave later.

What was it that Jen had said she wanted to learn about? That's right, it was that stuff about consciousness. The soul. The human mind. Where did the human mind come from? The Pembrokeshire trees and hedges are flashing past my window and for some reason I'm mulling over those same questions. What are we? Where have we come from? Why am I here in this body, living this life, seeing the world through these eyes, rather than someone else's? Does everyone else see the world the same as I do or do they see something totally different? I am truly glad that I am living the life I am though, rather than someone else's, because right now my life is absolutely brilliant!

Jen had talked about that Descartes guy and his theory that the mind was separate to the brain. And that the mind might possibly carry on existing after we die, somehow. Maybe I could come up with something worthwhile to say on that subject. Something that would impress her. Mind you, I'm guessing that this problem has puzzled the greatest human thinkers for thousands of years. The chances of me solving it before four o'clock today are probably a bit remote.

For some reason I find my own mind meandering back to that episode of *Star Trek* that had been on TV last night. The one where Captain Kirk had gone through the transporter and come out as two, different versions of himself. Now that was an interesting situation. How would that have worked out in terms of Captain Kirk's mind? His consciousness? The two versions of him couldn't both have the same mind, could they? Surely that wouldn't make sense. Thinking about it, neither of the copies were the original Captain, as he had been split, so to speak, with each copy possessing only some of his attributes. So yeah, that probably meant that each copy had a mind of its own and Kirk's original mind only came back after they had been recombined into just the one Captain Kirk.

And then I start wondering. Rather than splitting Kirk into two different versions, like in the show, what if it had been a straight replication process. So you had an original Captain Kirk and an identical copy. The original would still have Kirk's original mind, his original consciousness. But what about the copy? It would have *a* mind, certainly. One that had come into existence when the copy was created. But surely it couldn't be the *same* mind as the original?

Okay, I tell myself, let's try and think about this more critically. Like an actual philosopher might. Forget about Captain Kirk. Let's say instead that it's *my* body that has been replicated. Let's imagine that I am currently sat next to an exact, atom-by-atom copy of myself. An identical Adam Gunson.

Would such a thing be possible? To make such a replica of me you'd need to reproduce the position of every atom, every sub-atomic particle in my body. Now, all the different electrons and other particles in the universe are identical to each other. I know that because I remember Mr Charlton telling us in one of his science lessons. So making the replica me would just be a case of arranging all the right kinds of sub-atomic particles in the right places, yes?

So how would you do that? You'd need to start by measuring all the positions of the particles in the original me. It would be more involved than recording the locations of stones on a beach or measuring the speed of a river. You'd need to use some kind of computer. Something more powerful than Derek's ZX Spectrum, presumably. The computer would probably need a memory bank bigger than the Earth in order to process all that information. In practical terms it would not be possible. But in theoretical terms... maybe?

Okay, so let's assume it is possible. I have my identical replica of myself. The replica me is identical in every way. The external features, skin, hair, eyes, the scar on my leg from that primary school injury – they have all been perfectly reproduced. The internal organs, the heart and liver etc., all the same as the original. And so is the brain. And also the contents of the brain, because the replica me is identical, right down to the subatomic level. And if my memories are just a set of electrical charges inside my brain, much like the way a computer program is recorded on a tape, then the replica would have my memories as well. Yes, the replica would be an exact physical copy.

But what about his consciousness? What about his mind? He would have *a* mind. Of course he would. But it wouldn't be *my* mind. Because my mind is still inside my original body, not his. I'm still looking at the world through my eyes, not his. He would be a copy of me. But he wouldn't be *me*.

So following this through (assuming what I've said so far is right) does that mean that whatever it is that makes up my mind, my consciousness, is not reproducible by making a copy of my physical body? Does that mean that my mind, my soul, my spirit if you like, must necessarily be made of something other than physical matter? Something like quintessence. Just as that Descartes guy had said?

Wow! This feels like something big. This feels like a big philosophical idea. Have I just hit upon an actual thing? Have I, Adam Gunson, teenage geography student, just uncovered an important truth about the human mind? I reckon Jen is going to be impressed...

Chapter 13

The visit to the Llys-y-fran reservoir and dam played out exactly as you might have expected it to. We went there. We got out of the minibuses. We looked at it. We came back.

During the return journey I pay little attention to the passing scenery. My thoughts are buzzing with what lies ahead for me. I am constantly checking the time on my watch. Jen had said to meet her in the games room. At four o'clock. But the time is running down. Why can't Mr Gardner drive any faster? I'm a bundle of energy, desperate not to be late, desperate for her not to think I have stood her up.

After what seems like ages I begin seeing things out the window that I recognise, trees and buildings and road signs that I remember as being not too far from the hotel. I start to relax a bit more and eventually the two minibuses pull up and park at the side of the hotel. It's three thirty-five. There's just enough time to return to the room, get tidied up and grab a change of clothes.

I'm desperate to get moving but Mr Gardner tells us to gather round before we disperse. What does he want now? Can't it wait? 'The rest of today is free time,' he tells us, 'but my advice is you make good use of it by getting your hydrology work written up while it's all still fresh in your minds.'

The group filters into the hotel lobby. Most of the others head straight up the stairs to their rooms. I notice that Rob Northwood and Paul Armstrong have gone through to the games room. Will they still be there later when I'm meeting Jen? No, they'll probably take themselves off somewhere secret to have a smoke.

I swiftly climb the stairs, only to find Martin Vickers kicking his heels outside the door of our room. 'Seagrave's got the key,' he says.

'What? Where is he?'

'Dunno. Probably brown-nosing Gardner. You know what he's like, always sucking up to teachers.'

Where is Seagrave? Why can't he get a move on? Come on, I don't have time for this. Several times I hear boots ascending the stairs but each time it isn't him. Finally he appears, ambles over to our door with no sense of urgency whatsoever and unlocks it.

'Right then,' says Seagrave once we are inside. 'Best make a start on that hydrology work.'

'Sod that,' says Martin after discarding his clipboard. 'I'm off out.'

'Mr Gardner said it would be best if we got it done straight away.'

'Honestly Seagrave, You are such a wet. Do you have to be a total square the whole time? You probably do all your homework on the same day it's set, don't you.'

'And what's so bad with that?'

'Do you have any kind of life outside of the school?'

'Oh, why don't you just piss off. I don't need your help with this anyway. It's not like you've made any useful contribution to anything we've been doing this week...'

Leaving those two to their ongoing dispute, I empty my remaining clothes onto the bunk bed and thumb through what options I have available. I decide to switch my jeans for the only other trousers I have with me – a fleck-patterned pair with pleats at the waist and narrow cuffs at the ankles. I also have a light grey shirt that I haven't worn yet. My grey moccasins and some fresh white socks will complete the look. I wish I had brought more wardrobe choices but this will have to do. The moccasins have got a bit dusty. I give them a quick wipe down using the corner of the bedspread.

Change of clothes in hand, I head over to the bathroom. However, getting washed is hampered by there being no hot water. I suspect most of the girls have chosen this exact time to take showers and baths. Annoying, but I manage as best I can, getting washed and changed as quickly as possible.

I don't use aftershave so didn't bring any but I wish I had some now. Seagrave has left his bottle of Mandate on the top of the toilet cistern. Do I want to use that? I undo the cap and give it a sniff. No, I don't want to use that.

I check the time again. Almost four o'clock.

'Hey, where are you off to?' Seagrave has an ocean of paper spread out across the bed; he looks up as I open the door. 'You'd better not be leaving me to do all this.'

'Just off to post my postcard,' I tell him. 'Don't want to miss the post.'

I haven't written the postcard yet but I grab it anyway along with my anorak, slip on my moccasins and I'm out the door. I sling the anorak over my shoulder, attempting to exude an air of casualness, before heading down the stairs. Do I need to check myself again? No, I think I'm looking sharp enough.

The games room is currently empty. The Space Invaders cabinet has the start screen flashing on its display but there's no one playing. Another check of my watch. Three minutes past, She'll be here any time now. I'm really excited about seeing Jen again. Will she be impressed with my big philosophical idea? Or will she tell me I've got it completely wrong? Either way, I'm excited!

'Yo, pool table guy.'

I hear a voice calling from behind but it doesn't sound like Jen's voice. And when I turn around it isn't Jen I'm looking at, it's Leena. And Leena is not alone. Either side of her are two other girls. They are the two girls who were with Jen and Leena in the lobby last night. All three of them are sniggering. I am confronted by a wall of sniggering, yellow jumpers.

'You here to meet Jen?'

'Yes.'

'She's not coming.'

'Oh. Okay.'

'She sends her apologies. She's had to go somewhere. She asked us to give you a message.'

'Right.'

'She says she'll meet you up in her room later. Eight o'clock. Room Twenty-Nine. Second floor.'

One of the other girls chips in. 'We're her roommates,' she tells me. 'So we'll be sure to disappear and, you know, give the two of you some privacy.'

'Oh. Right,' I say, trying to sound assertive.

'She's looking forward to, like, seeing you up there.'

'Oh. Okay.'

There's another round of sniggering between them.

'You are going to treat her right, aren't you?' the third girl says, laughing.

'Sorry?'

'You're going to treat her nice, yeah?'

'Yes. Of course.'

"Cause if you're planning on, you know, having it off with her, you need to treat her proper, yeah?'

'Oh. Okay.' (Was I expecting that to happen? I'm fairly sure I wasn't.)

'Because Jen's our mate. You need to treat her right.'

'Of course.'

'We don't want you messing her about or causing her any grief.'

'N-no, of course not.'

'If you cause her any grief you'll have us to answer to.'

'O-okay.'

'And you know what you're doing, yeah?'

'Sorry?'

'You know how to do it with a girl, yeah?' The sniggering persists as a background to Leena's words.

'Y-yes,' I reply, unconvincingly.

'And you've got some johnnies?'

'Pardon?'

'Rubber johnnies. Durex. You've got some, yeah?'

'Because you don't want to be getting Jen pregnant,' one of the other girls chips in.

'N-no, of course not.'

'So have you got some johnnies?'

'Err... well, no.'

'Here. Better have this then.' Amid the rising chorus of giggles, Leena pushes a small cardboard item into my hands. 'There should be one good one still in there.'

'Oh. Thanks.'

'Make sure you use it.'

'Y-yes.'

'And there's nothing wrong with you, is there?'

'Wrong with me?'

'You don't have any kind of venereal disease?'

'No, of course not.'

'No AIDS, gonorrhoea or chlamydia?'
'No.'
'Hepatitis? Herpes? Syphilis?'
'Definitely not.'
'You'd better not have. Like I said, Jen's our mate.'
'And we don't want you giving her any kind of infection.'
More sniggering.
'So you got all of that? Room Twenty-Nine. Eight o'clock.'
'And don't stand her up. Yeah?'
'Yes. I mean, no. Of course.'

The three of them move off towards the lobby, sniggering and whispering to each other. Before they disappear up the stairs Leena glances back at me with a cold, mirthless sort of smile on her thin, dark lips. And I'm left there standing on my own with a used Durex packet in my hand and thinking, what? What the hell just happened? I was doing my best to maintain a calm, cool exterior but I'm certain that my face will have turned crimson with embarrassment. And my mind is now a chaos of emotions.

Did you think that was going to go the way it did? Hell, I certainly didn't. Obviously I had come down here with certain ideas about what would happen. I thought I'd be meeting Jen and that we'd probably go off somewhere. And I'd listen to her tell me more about philosophy and I was hoping to impress her with that idea that I'd had. And maybe, if I was lucky, there might be a bit of kissing and stuff. But I wasn't thinking that there would be, you know, anything more.

I mean, it's only our first date. Surely Jen wasn't intending that me and her were going to... was she? I think back to the way she had smiled at me before we parted. There was no indication that she had been thinking along those lines... was there? But why has Leena told me to meet Jen up in her bedroom? Why not the games room, or some other public area? What does that mean? Oh God! My head is spinning like a spin dryer with a whole laundry load of thoughts tumbling around inside. This is turning into a nightmare. A minute ago I couldn't wait to see Jen again, but now...

Okay, so I'll level with you. At this time in my life I know nothing about girls and I know nothing about sex. Despite all my affirmative mumblings during that interview with Leena just now, I know nothing. Jesus, I hadn't even kissed a girl before today. Okay, so I know slightly more about sex after watching *The Wicked Lady* last night but I still know basically nothing.

I cast my eyes over the Durex packet that I now have in my hand. Condition-wise, you would definitely have to describe this item as 'previously enjoyed'. The cardboard is creased and there is grime in the creases. This thing is dirty. I remember how, in the past, I would sometimes pick up another boy's toy and it would be dirty in a way that my own toys never were. This feels like that kind of dirty. Another boy's dirt. Who knows what hands it has previously passed through. Jesus, how has it suddenly come to this? How come I am now standing there like a jerk holding this piece of filth?

I've never handled a box of condoms before. I've never even seen one before. You have to remember that this is 1985. You can't just pick up a box of rubber johnnies from a supermarket shelf and pay at the self-service till. You have to buy them from the chemists. They are kept behind the counter. You have to ask for them. And at this time there's still a bit of stigma attached to them. I remember one of the kids at school being given detention after larking about with an inflated Durex during break time.

Actually, there is an alternative way of obtaining them. You can get them from the self-service machines in public toilets. There's one of those dispensers in the toilet in the hotel bar. I suspect that this item probably originates from there.

It looks and feels like a small cigarette packet, though obviously it isn't. The writing on the front says that it originally contained three but Leena had implied that it was no longer a complete set. I keep staring at the box, as if I'm expecting it to tell me something useful. Does the Durex packet have any advice on it? Any sage guidance for me in this time of stress? No, of course it doesn't

At Tangley Wood School, the closest thing we ever got to sex education were the moral improvement lessons we had in the fourth and fifth years. Well, I say lessons but they were really more like a set of lectures instructing us on how to live worthy lives. Old Mr Marlin, from the history department, was our teacher. Mr Marlin was a man of traditional views and his talks were guided by a strong Christian compass. As far as sex education went, Mr Marlin didn't tell us much and what he did tell us was a bit vague, a bit 'round the houses' as explanations of these things go. In fact, the only bit of those lessons that properly stuck in my mind were his warnings about the dangers of lewd thinking. I don't recall learning anything useful from those lessons. If Mr Marlin had told us any useful information about sex I am fairly sure I would have remembered it.

Oh this is ridiculous. Why am I getting myself into a state like this? I'm going to see Jen later and it's going to be brilliant. So what if I've had no experience before? She seems like an understanding girl, doesn't she? I will be going to meet her with absolutely no expectations. And as for anything else that may or may not happen while I'm with her... I'm trying not to dwell on it. It isn't easy though.

What should I do with the condom packet? I don't want it. It's so disgusting that I really ought to chuck it in the nearest bin. But there is no bin anywhere in sight. So instead I thrust it into my anorak pocket and turn to head back up to the room. Then I remember the postcard. I sit down at one of the video game tables. I can feel my hand shaking as I hastily write out a stilted message to my mum and dad. I address it to my home and apply the stamp to the right corner.

There's a letterbox for outgoing post on the front desk in the foyer. On my way back to the stairs I stop by the desk and slip the postcard in the letterbox. A part of me considers posting the Durex packet through the letterbox as well, just to get rid of it. But then I spot the hotel manager watching me from the back office. The eyes in that bowling ball head sear into me like I am some primitive life form that has just crawled in from the sea. I smile faintly back at him and hasten away.

Up in the hotel room I find that Martin and Seagrave have been continuing to needle each other. The catalyst for their current angst appears to have been Martin changing into an Iron Maiden tee-shirt.

'I don't know how you can listen to that rubbish,' says Seagrave cynically. 'That's not proper music. It's just noise.'

'You don't know what you're going on about,' says Martin. 'It's good stuff. Better than the bollocks music you listen to.'

'You don't know anything about the kind of music I listen to.'

'Okay then, try me. What's the last record you bought? Probably ABBA or some crap like that.'

'No it wasn't actually. It was Foreigner. And anyway, what's wrong with ABBA?'

'They're rubbish.'

'No they're not. Some of their stuff is really good.'

'Come on Seagrave, get with the times. No one listens to ABBA anymore.' Martin glances in my direction. 'Gunson, you agree, don't you?'

I'm expecting him to answer for me like he usually does, only this time he doesn't. I look at him and I look at Seagrave. The thing is, I like ABBA too. I actually once had the same conversation with Derek and Derek had also insisted that ABBA were not cool. But they did some brilliant songs that were and always will be fantastic. Their music is truly joyous. It's just that, for a brief period during the mid-1980s, ABBA happen to be a bit out of style.

'Martin's right.' I hear myself repeating the shameful words. 'No one listens to ABBA anymore.'

'Told you so,' says Martin. 'You need to be getting into some proper music.' He tugs and points at the front of his tee shirt. 'Iron Maiden, AC/DC, Motörhead, that's where the future of rock is.'

'No thanks,' says Seagrave dismissively. 'Of course, the truth is that there's very little decent new music around these days, anyway. And the person we can all blame for that is Mark Chapman.'

'Mark Chapman? Who's that?'

'Mark Chapman, you moron, is the man who murdered John Lennon.' Seagrave shakes his head in disbelief. 'I'm telling you, if Lennon was still alive then the Beatles would almost certainly be back together by now. And they'd be playing at the Live Aid concert too.'

'Oh I see, so that's your record collection, is it? ABBA and Foreigner and the Beatles?'

'I suppose you're going to tell me that you don't like the Beatles either?'

'That music is stone-age stuff. Like Beethoven and Mozart. No one listens to that anymore.'

Seagrave shakes his head again. 'Unbelievable. You, Vickers, are a total philistine. You know what my advice is? My advice is that you go out and buy yourself a copy of *Revolver* and listen to it four times uninterrupted. If you still don't like the Beatles after that then I'm sorry but there's no hope for you.'

Tonight's dinner is sausage casserole. In theory this is one of the tastier meals we have been served this week but in practice I am not digesting it well. From my place in the dining room I can see Jen. She's with the other Kimble College students, sat around their table on the far side of the room. She's got Leena on one side and that guy called Hughie on the other. I'm hoping to catch her eye when she gets up to collect her pudding from the side table. But she doesn't get up, she stays in her seat and one of the other girls fetches it for her.

I notice that Jen is very chatty with Hughie. I had previously wondered whether or not they might be boyfriend and girlfriend. Oh God, what if they are? What if I'm up in Jen's room and he comes in and finds us together? What if I end up getting into a fight with him? Or, even worse, what if a teacher comes in and finds the two of us alone together? I might find myself having to climb out onto the window ledge or hide in a box or something. Jesus, there are so many ways that it could all end up a total disaster...

The Kimble College students finish before us and they all file out the door. Jen turns her head and smiles at me as she passes. That smile again. I can't wait to be with her. Leena and those two other girls also glance sideways at me as they walk by. I do another quick time check. Six thirty. An hour and a half to go.

Back up in the hotel room, the tensions between Martin and Seagrave have escalated to a new height. Seagrave, of course, wants us to get on and complete the hydrology write-up.

'Bollocks to that,' says Martin. 'I'm going to the pub with Rob and Paul.'

'Yes, of course you are,' moans Seagrave. 'Why did you even bother coming back to the room? Just leave Adam and me to do the work. You're the one who'll be sorry. You're the one who'll get a rubbish exam grade. Anyway, the pub is out of bounds, remember? Mr Gardner is going to catch you down there and you're all going to get it in the neck.'

'Ha! Well that's where you're wrong. Because Gardner isn't here.'

'Yes he is. He was down in the dining room just now.'

'He was, but now he's gone. Both him and Lewis have left. Paul overheard them talking. Apparently Lewis has got some relatives who live nearby. They've both gone off in one of the minibuses to go see them.'

On hearing this Seagrave's face betrays a look of surprise, but his position remains unmoved. 'You still shouldn't go. It's wrong. They're trusting us all to not do anything stupid. It would be a betrayal of their trust.'

'Betrayal?' Martin laughs. 'Ha! That's rich that is, you talking about betrayal.'

'What do you mean by that?'

'You know what I mean.'

'Oh, so we're back to that again are we? That sodding sixth form party. How many times do I have to tell you? It wasn't me that complained to the school.'

'Yeah. Of course it wasn't.'

'I'm telling you, it wasn't me.'

Martin glares at Seagrave, his eyes brimming with hatred. 'Just look at you,' he spits. 'Standing there in your polyester lionels, carrying on like you think you're better than me. Two weeks ago you were in school uniform and now you're dressed like that. How can anyone be as square as you? You've gone straight from being a kid to being middle-aged.'

'I have no idea what you're talking about.'

'Seagrave, no one wears flared trousers anymore. They may have been fashionable ten years ago but they are not fashionable now and they will never be fashionable again.'

'They are not flared trousers,' Seagrave snaps back. 'And anyway, you're one to talk. At least my clothes are better than the crap fashion you wear.'

'What are you saying?'

'What I'm saying, Vickers, is that your clothes are rubbish. Filthy jeans. Filthy tee-shirts. An army jacket that makes you look like an Action Man. And as for those ridiculous boots...'

Martin takes great offence to this critique of his footwear. 'What the hell is it with you, Seagrave? Do you *want* to get your head kicked in? These boots, I'll have you know, are British Army standard. Flexible, comfortable, durable, waterproof, fitted with a steel toe cap. And guaranteed to kick the crap out of anyone who asks for it.'

'Oh yes that's right, go on, threaten me with violence. You wanna have a go? Come on then.'

'Well maybe I will,' Martin starts shouting angrily. 'Maybe I *will* kick your head in.'

'Come on then. Yeah, come on you Neanderthal, you ignorant cockface, you... you cretinous arsehole...'

'Hey don't feel you have to hold back, Seagrave. If you've got something to say to me then just come out and say it.'

'Crap, that's what you are, Vickers. Crap, crap, crap. Your clothes are crap, your hair is crap, your work is crap, your music is crap, your life is crap, EVERYTHING ABOUT YOU IS CRAP!!!'

'Hey, watch out.' Martin suddenly starts chuckling. 'You've just given yourself another nosebleed.'

'What?' Seagrave checks his face in the mirror on the wardrobe door. Sure enough, a small stream of blood has once again begun emerging from his right nostril.

'Oh great. You've done that. That's your fault, that is.' He turns and storms off into the bathroom.

'Stupid wanker,' Martin mutters. 'What a gimp. Anyway, you two boys will have to excuse me. I'm off to the pub. Hello, what's this?'

Martin's eyes have happened upon something on Seagrave's bed. Amongst all the sheets of scattered paper is an A4-sized notebook with a brown paper cover. Seagrave's diary. He has neglected to lock it away like he usually does. The word 'PRIVATE' on the front cover has captured Martin's attention. 'What have we here?' He thumbs through the pages. 'So he keeps a secret diary, does he? The bastard. Doubtless he's been writing stuff about me. What's the prick been saying then?' He flicks through until he reaches the last entry. He reads:

> *'Thursday April eleventh. Another miserable day on this bloody school trip. Everyone hates me here. Why do I have to be stuck spending every minute of the day and night in the company of people who hate me? Today I spent the morning standing in a freezing cold river and this afternoon we've got a totally pointless trip to a reservoir.*
> *I can't stop thinking about Roz. She was supposed to be here. Why isn't she here?'*

Martin stops reading. He looks at me, open-mouthed. 'Hey Gunson, you hear that? Seagrave fancies Roz! Seagrave fancies Roz Madsen! Ha!'

The bathroom door bursts open and Seagrave storms back into the room. He has toilet paper stuck up his nose and he is screaming with rage.

'How dare you! Give that back to me right now!' He tries to grab the diary back but Martin holds it above his head while chanting 'Seagrave fancies Ro-oz, Seagrave fancies Ro-oz' in that familiar nah-nah-nah-nah-nah nah sing-songy way.

And I'm stood there watching all this and thinking, what? What the hell is happening?

Chapter 14

Jealousy. It's a strange thing, jealousy. I've never thought of myself as being a particularly jealous person but it's curious how jealousy can creep up on you without you realising it.

During those two months I've spent not asking Roz to go out with me, there have been many uncomfortable times. The only lesson we have in common is geography and there have been a few times here and there where I've gone all day without seeing her. Those days were not good days. But worse than those have been the days where I've noticed her hanging out and chatting with other guys. I'm confident, from what I have observed of her around the school, that she doesn't have a current boyfriend. Derek thinks that as well. But, nevertheless, there have been times when I've seen her walking alongside other boys between lessons, or speaking with one of the trumpet players at the end of orchestra rehearsal in a suspiciously friendly manner. Worst of all, I once saw her at the far end of the playground during break time chatting with Paul Armstrong. Thoughts of her spending any kind of quality time with that libidinous fiend were not happy thoughts. She doesn't have a current boyfriend though. I'm sure of it.

Since meeting Jen I have barely thought about Roz at all. But suddenly I'm confronted by a new, bizarre truth – Stuart Seagrave is also interested in Roz. Is this what jealousy feels like? I'm not sure how I feel about Roz right now. But I don't like the idea that Seagrave fancies her. I don't like it at all.

Martin Vickers continues to chant, 'Seagrave fancies Ro-oz, Seagrave fancies Ro-oz.'

'Give me that.' Seagrave lunges at Martin but Martin avoids him. Drawing on whatever military skills he may have learnt, he jumps onto the double bed and slides across to the other side, sending all the sheets of paper flying. Seagrave scurries round the bed to intercept him but Martin continues to avoid capture. He bounds up the ladder to the upper bunk and pulls the ladder up after him.

'Give it back to me, Vickers. Give it back right now.'

'No. I want to see what else is in here.' He re-opens the diary at the page he was reading from before and continues:

'I can't stop thinking about Roz. Why isn't she here? She was supposed to be here. What a totally miserable life mine is at the moment. Stuck here in this wretched hotel room with Martin Vickers and

Adam Gunson. They all hate me. This is the worst birthday I have ever had.'

Martin pauses. A stiff silence falls upon us. 'What? Is today...' He looks Seagrave square in the face. '...is today your... birthday?'

'So what if it is?' says Seagrave sourly.

'As in, your seventeenth birthday?'

'Yes.'

'Hey, Seagrave, you should have said.'

'Why? So I could give you an excuse to wind me up even more?'

'N-no.' Martin looks at me, grasping for something to say. 'If we'd known it was your birthday we would've done something. Wouldn't we, Gunson?'

'Like what?' asks Seagrave. 'What would you have done?'

'If we'd known it was your birthday we'd have... we'd have not made you be the one who stood in that freezing cold river this morning.'

'Would you have done that? Really?'

'Well okay, maybe not that. But we'd have done something.'

Our talk is interrupted by a knock at the door. I open it as I'm nearest. It's Rachel Barrett. 'Alright, boys?' she says. 'Everything okay? I've come for your hydrology figures. Hey Stuart, what's happened to you?'

'What? Oh.' Seagrave removes the toilet paper from his nose. 'No, it's nothing.'

'You boys haven't been fighting, have you?'

'No, it was just a nosebleed. I'm all okay now.'

'Hey Rachel,' says Martin, climbing back down from the bunk bed, 'guess what?'

'What?'

'Please don't tell her,' I hear Seagrave plead.

'Don't tell me what?' I can see Rachel's ears prick right up at the chance of hearing some gossip. And I know why Seagrave's face is now filled with dread. Rachel Barrett is not discreet. If she gets wind of him fancying Roz then everyone will know about it by the morning.

Martin is still holding the diary. 'Seagrave...' He begins to speak while looking at Seagrave. Both he and I look at Seagrave's face, drained of all colour and with an expression that is begging Martin to say nothing. '...it's his birthday. Yeah, it's Seagrave's birthday today.'

'Is it your birthday today Stuart?' Rachel beams at him, 'Oh wow! Happy Birthday! You should have said. We'd have got you something.'

'He didn't tell any of us,' says Martin. 'We've only just found out.'

'So Stuart, you must be seventeen today then.'

'Yes,' Seagrave mumbles.

'Wow. Your seventeenth birthday is, like, a really big deal. Are you doing anything to celebrate?'

'Celebrate?' says Seagrave doubtfully. 'No.'

'You must. You must do something. We're all sneaking out to the pub this evening. You should come too.'

'Oh, I don't think so.'

'But you must. It's your seventeenth birthday. You have to do something to mark your seventeenth. Mr Gardner and Mrs Lewis have both gone off for the evening.'

'Yeah we heard that too,' says Martin.

'Julie saw them drive off in one of the minibuses about ten minutes ago. They've definitely gone. So there's no chance of being caught. You must come. Say you will?'

Rachel stays with us for a couple more minutes, exchanging numbers and figures from the morning's hydrology work. Before leaving she again urges Seagrave to join her and the other girls at the pub but he remains non-committal. 'Thank you, Vickers,' he says once Rachel has gone. This time there is a real glimmer of sincerity in his voice. 'Thanks for not telling her.'

'I did tell her it was your birthday.'

'No, I mean about the other thing. Thanks for not telling her about... Roz.'

'That's okay. I'm not the kind of bloke who likes to stir up girl gossip. Rachel's right though. A man's seventeenth birthday is something that has to be observed. If they're going down the pub then we should too.'

'We can't do that. Mr Gardner specifically told us not to. And we still have to finish the write-ups.'

'Bollocks to that,' says Martin. 'No, we have to go. You heard what Rachel said. She specifically invited you. You can't refuse. Look, Seagrave, you complain about people not liking you, yeah? Well the reason they don't like you is because you don't join in with stuff. If you joined in more then people would like you more.'

'But I don't want... I don't want to get into any kind of trouble.'

'Okay, listen to me,' says Martin. 'I'll tell you what my dad told me. He said that, when you're at school, the teachers are always telling you to stay out of trouble. Stay out of trouble, they tell you, and everything will be alright. Stay out of trouble and your life will be okay. But the truth is that that is all bollocks. Because when you're a man there will be times when you get into trouble. No matter how careful you are at avoiding trouble, there will be times when trouble finds you. And when trouble finds you, you need to know how to deal with it. At school they teach you maths and history and geography and crap like that, things that you are never going to need in life. But there is one thing that you need to know that they don't teach you at school. And that thing is how to deal with trouble.'

'Okay,' says Seagrave, doubtfully, 'so how do you learn to deal with trouble?'

'You learn to deal with trouble,' says Martin, 'by going out and finding it and staring it in the face. And that's what we're going to do tonight.'

'You mean by going to the pub?'

'Exactly.'

'I'm not sure. They probably won't serve us in there anyway.'

'Yes they will. I was in there with Rob and Paul on Tuesday. We had no problem getting served. Look, tell you what, we'll just go and have the one drink, to celebrate your birthday, to, you know, mark the occasion. And while we're there we can work out how to get Roz Madsen to go out with you. Gunson will help, won't you Gunson? Of course he will.'

Martin picks up his flak jacket and opens the door. Seagrave, having secured his diary and tidied up all the paper that was on the floor, follows him out. Is Seagrave really going to go to the pub with Martin? I can't believe that he is. I don't really want to go to the pub either, of course. I'm still thinking about my rendezvous with Jen that is, according to my watch, now one hour and ten minutes away. I would be happy to make my excuses now but I suspect Martin is going to insist on me coming. So I grab my anorak and leave the room behind them.

We make our way along the corridor, passing the rooms that are occupied by other members of our group. Before we reach the stairs Martin stops and knocks on one of the doors.

'What are you doing?' Seagrave whispers anxiously.

The door opens and Gemma Thorneycroft appears. She's wearing a pink bathrobe and her hair is wrapped up in a towel. 'Alright boys,' she greets us.

'We're off down the pub now,' says Martin.

'Yeah, Rachel told us. Hey Stuart, Happy Birthday. You should have said, we'd have organised something proper for you. I've just been washing my hair. Give us time to get ourselves fixed up, yeah? And we'll see you down there.'

Gemma shuts her door and we continue down the stairs and into the lobby. The manager is stood at the reception desk and notices us passing. 'You okay there, lads?' He looks us up and down with his usual suspiciousness.

'Yes fine thanks,' Martin replies.

'Where are you off to?'

'Oh nowhere, just going out to get a bit of fresh, seaside air.'

We make our way out through the front door. 'He's going to tell Mr Gardner,' says Seagrave with a voice full of panic. 'You could see it on his face. When Mr Gardner gets back he's going to tell him.'

'Will you shut up. No one's going to be telling anybody anything. It's all going to be fine.'

We walk through the front door of the hotel, out into the cool, evening air. It's close to sunset – the sun has almost completed its slow, fiery slide into the sea on the far horizon. The outside of the hotel is cloaked in gloom. A couple of lamps have now come on, highlighting the corners of the car park. I see a group of figures, their outlines hazy, emerge from behind the Kimble College minibus.

One of them calls out to us. 'Alright Martin.' It's Rob Northwood. Paul Armstrong is with him. It's obvious that they have been smoking. There is also a third figure present. It's hard to make him out but I think it's Hughie, the guy who I'm hoping isn't Jen's boyfriend. Rob and Paul walk over and join us. 'Watcha,' says Martin. 'We're off down the pub. It's Seagrave's birthday.'

'Oh, is it? Happy Birthday Seagrave.'

'You two coming?'

'Yeah, we'll join you there in a bit. Just sorting out a bit of something first. A bit of business with this guy.' He jabs his thumb in the direction of Hughie, who has stayed behind in the shadows.

Leaving those three to whatever they are up to, we head off along the seafront. We pass by the remains of the Cocktail Club where Jen and I were earlier. I'm really not liking the idea of leaving the hotel but it's too late to say anything now. I'm thinking that I'll just wait until we're inside the pub and Seagrave and Martin are with other people. Then I'll slip away and come back to meet Jen. I doubt they'll even notice I've gone.

There is nobody else about, we have the whole of the seafront to ourselves. Martin is now in an ebullient mood – as we continue along the promenade he is swinging his left arm around each lamp post in turn. Seagrave though is having second thoughts. 'I'm really not sure about this,' he whines. 'It doesn't feel right. Come on, let's go back.'

'Will you relax, for Christ's sake,' says Martin. 'Look, we're almost there. The pub's just round that corner.'

'Who's that?' Seagrave points at a shadowy figure visible just ahead of us, alongside the promenade railings. In the failing light I can't make out who it is but, on seeing the three of us on the pavement opposite, it changes direction and starts moving speedily towards us.

'Oh God, it's Mr Gardner,' cries Seagrave, each of his gangly limbs now quivering with panic. 'That's it, we're all done for.'

The figure moves closer and closer until we can recognise its face. And it isn't Mr Gardner at all. It's Isaac.

'What are you lot doing?' he asks.

'We're going to the pub. It's Seagrave's birthday.'

'Oh, nice. Happy Birthday Stuart.'

'What are you doing out here?'

'Checking out the sky,' says Isaac. 'Looking out for, you know, any unexplained phenomena. It's like I've been telling Adam, this place is slap bang in the centre of the Welsh Triangle.'

'The Welsh Triangle?'

'Yeah, that's right,' Isaac continues. 'One of the centres of UFO activity.'

'Okay,' says Martin doubtfully, 'so you're out here searching the sky for, what, UFOs?'

'Correct.'

'Have you seen any?'

'Nothing so far. But there have definitely been some weird vibes going down the whole time we've been in this place. Have you been sensing it too? I get the feeling that something pretty big is going to happen tonight. Something pretty massive, I reckon.'

'Well that's good to know,' says Martin, 'but us three blokes have got an appointment to keep in the real world. We're going to the pub.'

'Oh, okay,' says Isaac. 'I'll come along too.' As we continue our path along the road Isaac starts walking beside me. 'This is good, meeting you like this,' he begins. 'I have news. I have made an important discovery. About that conspiracy I was telling you about.'

Great, I'm thinking. Marvellous. Another thing that I can totally do without tonight.

The four of us make our way across the road and round the corner to where the pub is. Seagrave pleads with Martin to not tell everyone they meet that it's his birthday. And his nerve is continuing to fail him – by the time we reach the entrance to the pub he has tried a further two times to turn around and go back.

Chapter 15

When I was younger I would often accompany my dad on his weekend trips into Woking or Camberley. My dad has only ever had one interest outside of work and that is horseracing. Or more specifically, betting on horseracing. And the main reason for my dad going into town was in order to go to the betting shop. I was too young to go in the betting shop myself, so I would have to hang around in the street outside, waiting for him. By the time I was sixteen I was finally old enough to enter the betting shop and I remember that first time going inside. And while I was inside that betting shop, even though I was now legally allowed to be there, I was gripped by a very strong feeling that this was still a place where I was not supposed to be.

I had the same feeling last year in Manfreds night club when I had managed to get into the sixth form party. And I'm feeling it again now as Martin Vickers, Stuart Seagrave, Isaac Lee and myself walk through the doorway of the Admiral Totty pub. Not just because we are all younger than eighteen, not just because we had been told very specifically not to leave the hotel, but also because the general ambiance of the place is not one of welcome. As we make our way inside, every face present turns and stares at us. And every one of those faces seems to be telling me, this is not a place where you should be.

'Right, I'll get the beers in,' says Martin. 'Seagrave, got any money?'

'What, seriously?' says Seagrave. 'Do you not have any?'

'No.'

'Honestly, Vickers, you are such a juvenile. Did you not think about that before you dragged us all in here?'

'I've got some,' I tell them, pulling out the change I have in my trouser pocket. Isaac helps out too, adding some coins from a small, brown purse he has produced from inside his overcoat.

'Cool. Lager okay for everyone?' Martin doesn't wait for an answer, he just struts straight over to the bar.

'He's wasting his time,' says Seagrave. 'Look at this place. We're never going to get served.' The panicky expression on Seagrave's face betrays the fact that, like me, he also feels that he very much shouldn't be in here.

'Let's sit over there.' Isaac points to an empty table in one of the corners, next to a grimy mirror.

I cast my eyes around the inside of the pub. It's smoky and murky and decorated with various souvenirs of the sea – fishing nets and lobster pots and bits of dried up starfish. There are old lengths of rope hanging from the nicotine-stained ceiling. There's a fireplace, not currently lit, with a pair of pirates' cutlasses fixed to the wall above. And watching over the table we're heading towards is a portrait of an ancient military man who I take to be the titular Admiral Totty. The face in the portrait also seems to be warning me off, confirming my own view that I shouldn't be there. In the years to come I will encounter many dingy drinking venues but this place will always be right up there as one of the most unwelcoming.

I take a seat at the table with Isaac beside me and Seagrave on a stool opposite. Martin is still at the bar, waiting to be served, that flak jacket of his looking rather out of place among the locals. And then I spot Chas Browning and some others from our group come in. They join Martin at the bar.

I check my watch again. Seven fifteen. It only took us about five minutes walking from the hotel to get here. As long as I am out of here by quarter to, all should be well. Once more of the Tangley Wood crowd are in here it will be easy for me to slip away.

I am aware that Isaac is cosying up to me on the bench. Here we go. I just know that this isn't going to be good. 'Right,' he begins, his eyes dripping with conspiracy theory madness, 'remember what I was telling you about before?'

'Remind me.'

'You know, about the blast furnaces.'

'What's this?' Seagrave asks.

'Do you remember, Stuart, when we were driving here on the motorway and we went past the blast furnaces at Port Talbot?'

'Yes. What of it?'

'And did you not notice that the real blast furnaces looked nothing like the diagram?'

'Diagram? What diagram?'

'The blast furnace diagram. You know, the picture we've been made to copy out in class all those times.'

'You mean the diagram that shows how the blast furnace operates?'

'Yeah.'

'What about it?'

'Were you not at all suspicious that the diagram we copied out all those times looks nothing like a real blast furnace.'

'Suspicious?' asks Seagrave. 'Why would it make me suspicious? The diagram is just a diagram. A model. A simplification. You wouldn't expect it to look exactly like the real thing.'

'Ha! That's what they want you to think. But I'm onto their secret. Look, I have a copy of the diagram here.' And from his overcoat he produces a sheet of A4 paper. He unfolds it to reveal a copy of the familiar iron and steel blast furnace diagram...

Fig 1.

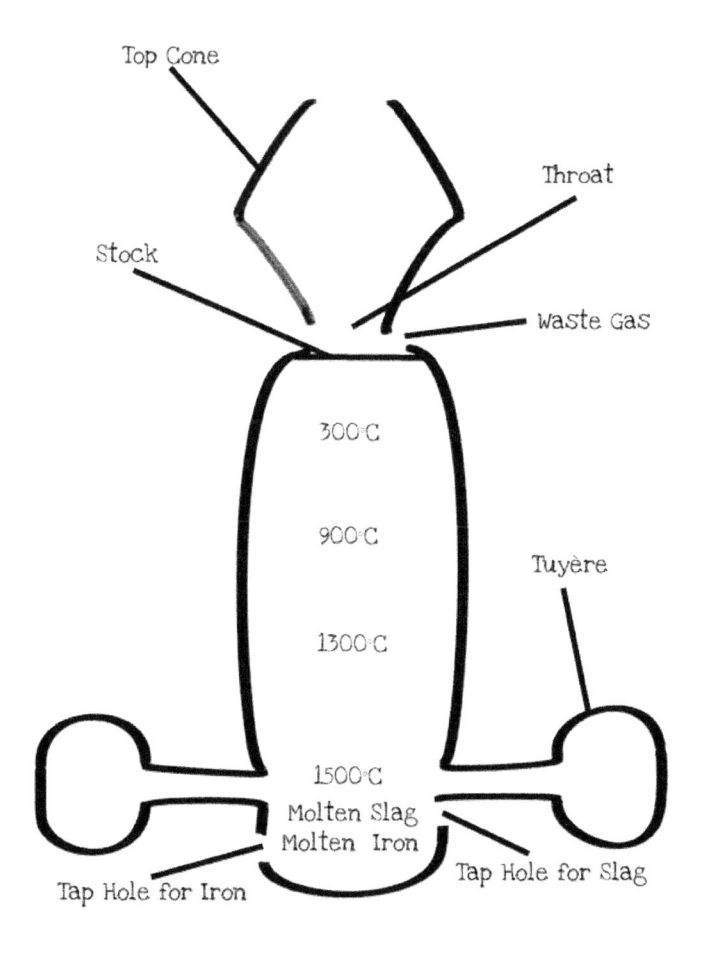

'Have you never wondered,' Isaac goes on, 'about all the different times we've been made to draw this diagram? All the different lessons it's come up in. In geography we do primary industry and we're made to draw the blast furnace diagram. In history we do the industrial revolution and we draw the same diagram. In chemistry we do the chemical composition of iron – same diagram. In physics we do the atomic structure of metals – same diagram. In design technology we do the manufacture of steel – same diagram. All these different lessons throughout our entire time at school and the teachers are making us draw this same picture, time and time and time again. Does that not make you at all suspicious?'

Seagrave and I look at each other. We have no idea where Isaac is going with this.

'It's always the same picture. And we're told that it's meant to be a diagram of a blast furnace. But it looks nothing like the real ones we saw from the motorway. And it's always drawn the same way. These things on the sides, the tuyères, they are always depicted like this with these round bits on the end. All these different lessons where we've been made to draw the exact same thing. And then there's biology – '

'Biology? Now come on, we've never drawn a copy of the blast furnace diagram during a biology lesson.'

'You think?' says Isaac. He takes the diagram and turns it upside down and scratches out all the labels with a pencil. And he's about to start relabelling the diagram but then, suddenly, Martin is back at the table, his hands carrying four pints of lager. Isaac quickly tucks his diagram away.

'Here you go.' Martin passes one of the glasses to each of us. The glasses are those bubble-sided tankard ones with handles. He sits on the stool next to Seagrave and it's clear that he intends on getting straight on with things. 'Right then, first item: Happy Birthday Seagrave.' Martin, Isaac and I raise our glasses. 'Second item: so you fancy Roz then?'

'Oh come on,' Seagrave pleads. 'You don't have to tell everyone.'

'What's this?' asks Isaac.

'Seagrave fancies Roz.'

'Okay,' says Seagrave. 'Fine. Yes, I admit it. I fancy Roz Madsen. There. Happy?'

Martin sips his beer before replying. 'Fair play to you, Seagrave. To be honest, I always thought you were, you know, not into girls.'

'What makes you say that?'

'Well, you just never seem to show any interest. And you didn't appear to think much of *The Wicked Lady* last night.'

'Yes, well not all of us are like you, Vickers. Just because I don't spend the whole time staring at women's breasts doesn't mean I don't have feelings.'

'No, no of course not. No, fair play to you, Seagrave. You fancy Roz. That's great. I wouldn't go out with her myself, of course.'

'Why? Because you won't go out with any girl that goes to our school?'

'Yeah, that's true. Plus she's a ginger. Not my type. My dad always told me never to trust people with ginger hair. And she has that snooty way with her. Aloof. Superior. Always going around with her nose stuck up in the air. Always looking at you like you're a piece of crap. And she hangs about with that poncy music room bunch. That poser Derek Hotchkiss and all that crowd from the school orchestra. I used to do biology lessons with her. I remember the way she went about dissecting that dead rat. Very clinical. I wouldn't want those hands touching me. But hey, that's just my opinion. If you think she's the girl for you then go for it. And to be fair, she does have nice tits.'

'Don't talk about her like that,' says Seagrave.

And I'm sat there thinking the same thing. Okay, so it's true that I'm not entirely sure how I feel about Roz right now. But I'm not liking this conversation. I'm not liking it at all.

'Are you going to ask her out then?'

'I don't know,' says Seagrave. 'If I do ask her she'll most likely say no. And then she'll tell all her friends and it'll get round the whole school and I'll be totally humiliated. And I don't want that, obviously.'

Martin slurps his lager. 'Well quite frankly,' he goes on, 'I'm surprised that you are worried about being humiliated. You're already the most ridiculed boy in the whole school. A bit more ridicule is not going to make a great deal of difference. So you're not going to ask her out then?'

'Oh, I don't know what to do. I was thinking about asking her during the field trip. In a way I'm a bit relieved that she's not here. Gives me an excuse not to go through with it.'

'Yeah, Roz was supposed to be here with us, wasn't she? Does anyone know why she isn't here?' We all shake our heads. 'One of the girls will know. I'll ask them when they get here.'

'It's a waste of time anyway. She'd never go out with me.'

'Oh I don't know about that. Roz's family are quite posh, aren't they. Her dad's an executive with an oil company or something, isn't he? I reckon you'd fit right in.'

'Okay then,' Seagrave snaps back at Martin. 'If you know so much about it, what do you suggest I do?'

'What would I suggest? Well let me think...' Martin sips more beer, considering the problem. 'Well first of all you need to sort your image out. Lose those polyester trousers for a start. Get yourself some decent clothes, I know you like to think that what you're wearing is okay but, trust me, the rest of us don't. You need to be a bit more with it. Less of a square. Make yourself look more like a bloke that a girl would want to be seen with.'

'Okay.' Seagrave seems unsure about the advice but, arms folded, carries on listening. 'Anything else?'

'Yeah, you want to try and get yourself in with the crowd she hangs out with. That school orchestra bunch. Do you play a musical instrument?'

'I used to play the trombone at my old school.'

'Well there you go then. Get yourself over to the music room and say that you're a trombone player and you'd like to join the orchestra. Easy. Then once you're in there doing the tromboning thing you'll have the perfect opportunity to chat her up.'

It's actually not a bad plan. It's similar to the one I had considered myself. And I know for a fact the orchestra is short of trombonists. But obviously I say nothing.

'Yeah, and another thing you can do,' adds Martin, 'is to have a party at your home. A seventeenth birthday party. Throw a party and invite us to it, obviously, and Roz of course. And then you'll have an excellent chance of getting off with her. It should help make you more popular with the rest of the school as well. It'll make up for you grassing on the sixth form party.'

'How many times do I have to tell you? It wasn't me that did that.' Seagrave has suddenly become guarded again. 'And I can't have a party at my home. There's no way I can do that.'

'Why not?'

'Because I just can't.'

While all this has been going on several of the girls, with Gemma Thorneycroft in the lead position, have entered the pub. They spot us and head straight over,

'Happy Birthday Stuart.'

'Happy Birthday Stuart.'

'Happy Birthday.'

There is a whole chorus of happy birthdays from the girls.

'We'll get you a drink. What're you having?'

'I'm fine for the moment, thanks.' Seagrave has barely touched the pint of lager in front of him.

'He'll have a vodka,' says Martin.

'Good choice!' says Gemma. 'One vodka for the birthday boy coming right up.'

'Let's make it a double,' adds Rachel. 'Something from all of us.'

'What did you tell them that for,' moans Seagrave after they have gone to the bar. 'I can't be drinking vodka.'

'Oh come on Seagrave,' says Martin. 'You're seventeen now. You need to start drinking proper drinks. Hey, and that's another thing. Now you're seventeen you can start driving lessons. Get yourself a driving licence and a car. Then you'll be well sorted for asking Roz out and taking her off somewhere.'

Seagrave stares gloomily down at the froth in the top of his pint glass. 'That's never going to happen. None of it's ever going to happen.'

'Why not?'

'Because...' He looks blankly at each of us in turn and then looks back at Martin. 'Because my family can't afford it. Because my family don't have any money to pay for driving lessons for me. And as for buying me a car, there's no chance.'

'What do you mean? I thought your family were well off. '

'Yeah.' Seagrave's eyes gaze blankly off towards some imagined distance. 'Well you think that because I probably gave all of you that impression. I try and give everyone that impression. But it isn't true.'

'I thought your dad had a job in London,' says Isaac. 'A stockbroker or something.'

'He did. He used to. But that was years ago. The firm he was with went bust and he lost all his money. And now he doesn't have a job. Yeah, that's right, my dad is unemployed. Has been for five years now. How do you think I came to end up at Tangley Wood Comprehensive School? When my parents still had the money I used to go to a private school. But after my dad lost his job they couldn't continue paying for me to go there. That's why I ended up at the same school as you lot. So no, Vickers, there is definitely no chance of my parents buying me a car or paying for driving lessons. It was actually touch and go as to whether they could even afford for me to come on this field trip.'

Gemma comes back to the table with a big glass of white wine in one hand and a brimming shot glass in the other. 'There you go Stuart.' She plops the shot glass down in front of him. 'That's from all of us.' She doesn't linger though, she returns to the noisy centre of the pub where everyone else is gathered.

Seagrave stares at the small glass of vodka. I'm guessing that he's going to push it away and refuse to drink it. To my surprise (and probably everyone else's too) he picks it up, looks at it for a moment and then gulps it straight down in one go.

'Wow,' says Martin. He looks as surprised as I've ever seen him. 'Okay, so you had to leave your old school because your parents could no longer pay the fees.'

'Yes that's right,' says Seagrave. 'You know what? I remember the day when I first found out I would have to leave that school. I can remember it as clearly as anything. I was in a history class and one of the ladies from the school office came to the door and said the headmaster wanted to see me. What does the headmaster want with me, I thought. Was I in trouble or something? So I went along to his office and he looked at me and said that he understood I was going to be leaving the school. And I told him no, I'm not leaving the school, I didn't know anything about that. So he said okay and let me go. And then that evening my mum and dad came over to me and said I might have to leave the school. Because they couldn't afford to pay the fees anymore. And they asked me how I felt about that. And I remember exactly what I said. I said that I would like to stay there if I could. I actually said I would like to stay there. But you know what? I absolutely hated that school. It was a horrible place. I had no friends there, especially during that last year. All the other boys hated me. They all kept on having a go at me.

'And d'you know something else? The school put me on the dining room cleaning rota for a second time. I'd already done it once. I'd already been on that cleaning rota. I had assumed that it was a rota and everyone took it in turns to do it. But no, the next term came around and I was still on the rota. I was the only one in my class who was still on it. At the time I thought it must have been a mistake, but thinking back on it I know what was going on. They did that deliberately. They kept me on that cleaning rota because my parents were behind with the fees.'

Seagrave's eyes are now filling with bitter remembrance. He wipes his hand across his mouth, downs a gulp of lager and continues. 'And another thing. The meals they served you at that school were vile. Absolutely disgusting. No wonder my guts are in such a state after years of eating that food. And to think that my parents were paying for it. Paying money that they couldn't afford for me to eat that crap. Unbelievable. And d'you know the worst thing? One of the so-called meals they served us was coleslaw. Or at least they called it coleslaw. But it was actually just bits of raw shredded carrot and cabbage. It was revolting. I hated it. And because I hated it I told everyone that I hated coleslaw. But you know what? It turns out that actual coleslaw isn't like that at all. Actual, proper coleslaw is made with mayonnaise and is really delicious. All that time I'd spent telling people I didn't like coleslaw and it turns out the stuff I didn't like wasn't coleslaw at all.'

Seagrave gulps down a further gulp of beer while the rest of us sit there, looking at our hands, in a slightly stunned silence.

'Christ, Seagrave,' says Martin after a pause. 'I'm sorry, I had no idea. I thought that your family was, you know, well off.'

'Well we're not well off. We're a long way from being well off. We don't even have a proper home at the moment. We're living in temporary accommodation. In a house the council has provided for us. You wanted to know the reason why I can't have a party, why I can't invite anyone round to my home. Well that's the reason. You think I don't want to have a party? You think I don't want to invite people round. I wish I could do that more than anything. But it's just not possible. And I know you all think that it was me that complained to the school about the sixth form party, but it wasn't. It wasn't me.'

Another silence falls over the group – it lasts for about ten seconds before Martin again breaks it. 'Bloody hell Seagrave, I had no idea things were like that for you. But hey, you'll be alright. You're a smart kid. You're clever. You'll get those good A Level results you keep on about and you'll go to university and all that. You'll be okay.'

Seagrave's head drops and he stares down at his beer. 'Yeah, that's what all the teachers tell my parents during parent evenings. "Stuart is bright," they say, "Stuart is clever, Stuart does well in the class." Well you know what? I'm not so sure being clever is such a good thing. As far as I can tell, all being clever does is let you see how rubbish and horrible the world really is.'

'Oh come off it,' says Martin firmly. 'Don't give me that. Pull yourself together. You're seventeen. You've got your whole life to look forward to. It's not as if your best coleslaw-eating days are already behind you. Like I said, you just need to get yourself some better clothes and make yourself look a bit less like a gimp. Then people will start treating you like a regular kid and Roz Madsen may even agree to go out with you. And if your parents have got no cash then you need to deal with it. Get yourself a weekend job. Get your own money. Look, I'm sorry to hear about all the crap you've had to put up with and I'm sorry if I've been giving you a hard time. But you do tend to set yourself up as a bit of a target. For Christ's sake, if you don't like people winding you up then don't walk around with a key sticking out of your back.'

But Seagrave remains unpacified. 'Why bother?' he says. 'Let's be honest, Roz is never going to want to have anything to do with someone like me. Look at me. It's pathetic. I'm not even the main character in my own story.'

Martin and Isaac and I look at each other and we're all thinking the same thing.

'I think Seagrave might be pissed,' says Martin.

'I guess he's not used to drinking,'

'Excuse me,' says Seagrave, 'I am not pissed.'

'I think you might be. Just a bit.'

I can see where Martin is coming from. In my experience there are two types of drunk people, the ones who get happy and excited when drunk and the ones who get all sad and depressed. Seagrave would appear to be of the second type.

'I can't be pissed,' insists Seagrave. 'I haven't drunk hardly anything. Just that vodka Gemma gave me and some lager.'

'I think the vodka Gemma gave you was a double,' says Isaac.

'Yeah, it was.' says Martin. 'Plus the vodka I put in your lager at the bar may also be a factor.'

'What the hell!' Seagrave shouts. 'You put vodka in my lager? What did you do that for?'

'It's your birthday. I wanted you to have a good time. Hmm, hasn't really worked though, has it?'

Chapter 16

My watch is telling me the time is seven forty-five. I really want to be back at the hotel now with Jen. But I am not at the hotel, I am stuck in the Admiral Totty pub drinking a pint of lager. I don't even particularly like lager; I don't care much for the taste of it, I only drink it because everyone else drinks it. And rather than looking at Jen's beautiful face, I am looking at Stuart Seagrave. For a while there he was getting so stressed with Martin that I thought he was going to have another nosebleed. But his face is now white and sickly-looking. I am face to face with the sick man of Shore Haven.

Chas Browning, beer in hand, has joined us at the table. 'You boys okay?' he asks. 'You alright there, Stuart? You look a bit pale, mate.'

'It's his birthday,' says Martin. 'He's been enjoying a birthday drink. Haven't you, Seagrave?'

'I think I'm going to throw up,' says Seagrave. 'Where's the toilet?'

'You don't want to be using the toilet in this place,' says Chas. 'I was in there just now. It's bad. You really don't want to be going in there.'

'I'll go outside then. Where's the door?' Seagrave gets up sharply, knocking his stool over in the process. With his right hand clutching his stomach he urgently forces himself through the assembled bodies and cigarette smoke. Almost all the Tangley Wood students are now present, merrily gathered around Gemma and the other girls. 'You alright, Stuart?' they all laugh as he pushes his way to the door. 'You having a nice birthday?'

'The bloke can't take his drink,' observes Martin. 'That's another thing they ought to be teaching us at school. Drinking skills.'

About five more minutes pass. Some of the Kimble College students have now entered the pub as well, including Leena and those two girls from earlier. Jen isn't with them. They haven't spotted me, not yet at least. I really want to get out of this place.

'D'you think we should go and check on Seagrave?' I ask. 'To make sure he's okay?'

Martin considers the question as he swallows the dregs of his pint. 'Yeah, we probably should,' he says, a trace of conscience seeming to dawn on his face. 'Come on.'

We both get up and move towards the door. As I leave I give a quick glance over my shoulder. Leena still hasn't seen me, That's good. I notice that Isaac hasn't followed us, he's stayed sat at the table. He's now talking to Chas and his drawing of the blast furnace diagram has reappeared.

Outside it is now night time. There are no lights in the street where the pub is and it's hard to make anything out in the blackness. There's no sign of Seagrave. 'Where the hell is he?' Martin asks. But then we spot him. He's down on the seafront at the end of the road, still clutching his belly, one shoulder propped against a lamp post.

I can feel the wind blowing as the two of us hasten towards Seagrave's location. Which way is the wind blowing? I remember from geography lessons that the wind on the coast blows one way during the day and the other way during the night. But which way round is it? Does the wind at night-time blow towards the sea or towards the land? I really ought to remember that. If Seagrave is going to throw up we need to know which direction he needs to be pointing in.

'How are you feeling?' asks Martin when we get to him. Seagrave has repositioned himself against the railings overlooking the beach, his face now emptied of all remaining colour.

'I think I'm okay now,' says Seagrave. 'The nausea seems to have passed.'

'Hey, you'd better not start chucking up in front of me. If you feel the need to yawn the technicolour yawn, do it in that.' Martin points at a nearby litter bin that has an advert for Corona Cherryade on the side.

'Thank you, but I think I'm okay now.'

'If you want to head back to the hotel,' I offer, 'then I don't mind coming with you.'

'Thanks. Yes it's probably best if I head back.'

'No problem,' says Martin. 'There's no shame in it. Some blokes just can't handle being pissed.'

'Excuse me, I am not pished.'

'Yes you are.'

'No I'm not.'

'Yes you are. Look at you. You're slurring your words, you can't stand up straight and your eyes look like a couple of pickled onions. You're pissed.'

'I am not...' Seagrave insists. 'What I am is suffering from alcohol poisoning. I... I... I'm going to be sick...'

That is just excellent. Gazing down the road I can see our hotel, the black triangle of its roof silhouetted against the night sky. Somewhere inside there is Jen, waiting for me. I should be in there with her now, not stuck out here with an inebriated Seagrave. And then I see a figure on the other side of the road, running in our direction. The figure is heading towards the pub but, on seeing us, crosses over. It's Colin Winchester.

'What are you lot doing here?' he asks. 'What's the matter with Stuart?'

Seagrave has followed Martin's advice and is currently being sick in the litter bin. It is a truly revolting sight to witness.

'He's pissed,' says Martin.

'I am not pissed,' says Seagrave, retrieving his head from the bin. 'I have alcohol poisoning.'

'Yeah, right,' says Colin. 'Good luck with that. Anyway, you lads need to get yourselves back to the hotel. All hell's kicking off.'

'Why? What's happened?'

'Rob Northwood and Paul Armstrong have been caught smoking cannabis.'

'What?'

'They were smoking a joint in the car park. Them and one of the guys from the other school. The teacher from the other school caught them. And that teacher told the hotel manager and he's now reported it to the police.'

'Jesus!'

'Yeah. And he's contacted Gardner and Lewis and they're now on their way back too. I'm off to the pub to warn everyone. We all need to get back to our hotel rooms before Gardner and Lewis get back.' And with that Colin turns and hastens off towards the Admiral Totty.

'Bloody hell,' says Martin. 'Bloody, bloody hell.'

This is not good. Mind you, Rob Northwood and Paul Armstrong, they had it coming to them. Especially if they were dumb enough to get themselves caught smoking dope.

'Oh God!' Seagrave starts spiralling into a panic. 'I knew this was going happen. Didn't I tell you so? We're all going to get caught. We're all going to get caught and sent home. I knew I should never have agreed to any of this.'

'Shut up, Seagrave. No one's gonna get caught and no one's gonna get sent home, okay?'

'Do I smell of alcohol? I do, don't I. Mr Gardner's going to catch us and he'll know we've been drinking. This is a disaster.'

'For God's sake, just calm down, will you.' Seagrave is now starting to hyperventilate. Martin attempts to reassure him but with limited success. 'You don't smell of alcohol, okay? You smell of sick but you don't smell of alcohol. Now come on, we need to get back to our hotel room as quick as we can. We need to run. You're able to run, aren't you, Seagrave?'

I remember seeing Seagrave during games lessons and I know for a fact that he can't run. He couldn't run during games lessons and the pissed version of Seagrave does not appear to be any better at running than the sober one. But somehow the three of us manage to get quickly back to the hotel.

We have just made it as far as the Cocktail Club building, opposite the entrance to the car park, when I spot some headlights approaching from the right.

'Quick,' says Martin. 'Take cover.' He drags us all down to the ground, behind the low, sandy wall at the side of the Cocktail Club. And his instincts prove to be good as, from that position, we can see that those headlights belong to the green Tangley Wood minibus. We watch as it slows down, turns into the carpark and jerks to a halt. The headlights go out, the engine stops and two figures appear on either side. The recognisable shapes of Mr Gardner and Mrs Lewis. They walk urgently up to the hotel porch and enter the front door.

'You two stay here,' whispers Martin. 'I'll check and see if the coast is clear.' He slips away, crossing the road in a crouching run, his body close to the ground. In the present state of darkness you could easily mistake his movements for those of a fully trained SAS commando. Once in the car park he shuffles to the right, keeping in the shadows, creeping slowly round the stationery cars towards the porch.

Seagrave, crouched beside me, is becoming ever more panicked. 'This is it,' he mutters over and over. 'We're done for. We're all done for.' And my own heart is racing too. I am not enjoying this. There are some people who seem to love taking risks, some people, like Martin over there, currently inching his way round the side of that Morris Marina, who seem to embrace danger and lap up the rush of dopamine that goes with it. But I am not one of those people. I'm almost as panicked by our current peril as Seagrave is.

From our location I can see the whole front of the hotel. Some of the windows have lights on inside. One of those windows on the second floor must be Jen's bedroom. She'll be in there now, expecting me. What's the time now? Seven minutes past eight. She'll be wondering where I am. She'll be thinking I've stood her up. She'll be thinking I've given her the elbow.

I can hear noise from down the road to my left. The rest of the school group are now hastening their way back from the pub. And then there's movement inside the glass front door of the hotel. It opens and Mrs Lewis appears. She has a firm, purposeful look about her. She doesn't look at all mumsy anymore. Is she going to spot Martin? No, he has tucked himself behind the rubbish bins, outside of her line of vision, and she doesn't see him. She struts out of the car park and down the road towards where the other voices are coming from.

Martin signals to us. 'Come on, the coast is clear.'

I wait until the back of Mrs Lewis is about ten yards away before shuffling swiftly across the road to join Martin. I'm concerned that Seagrave has become too paralysed with fear to move but, on turning, I see that he has followed me over, right on my heels.

Martin sneaks into the porch and peers through the glass in the door. 'The lobby's empty,' he says. 'We just need to get through and up the stairs without anyone seeing us. Are you both okay with that?'

'Yeah,' I nod. (Am I okay? Not really.)

'You okay with that Seagrave? You're not too pissed to manage it? Right, let's move.'

We make our way slowly through the door and into the hotel lobby. Martin is point man, Seagrave second, me bringing up the rear. We're all holding our breaths as, with knees bent and heads bowed low, we slowly make our crab-like way across the lobby. I glance at the reception desk. There's no one in sight. We're almost at the stairs now, it actually looks like we might –

'You three! Stop right there!'

We stop and turn our heads. It's Mr Gardner. Glaring down at us from the entrance to the bar.

'Stand up. '

The three of us stand up.

'Where have you been? Why aren't you up in your room?'

We shuffle round to face him, with Seagrave sandwiched between Martin and me.

'W-we've just been outside, Sir,' Martin offers. 'Getting some fresh air.'

'L-looking at the sky,' I chip in.

'Yeah that's right, we've been looking at the sky, Sir. Did you know, Sir, Shore Haven is in the middle of the, what's it called?'

'The Welsh Triangle.'

'Yeah, the Welsh Triangle. A known area for UFO activity.'

'Hush up,' says Mr Gardner. 'I'm not interested in any nonsense.'

'No Sir.'

Mr Gardner is absolutely fuming but there's also a flicker of panic in his eyes. I'm guessing he's never had to deal with a situation like this before. That beard is bristling, though, and his eyes are searing into us like laser beams. I sense that he might explode at any moment. There have been some truly horrendous volcanic eruptions over the years (e.g. Krakatoa, 1883) and Mr Gardner looks like he's about to blow in a way that will place him right up there with the worst of them.

'A short time ago Robert Northwood and Paul Armstrong were discovered out in the car park smoking drugs. Do you three know anything about that?'

'No Sir,' we each mumble in response.

'What did I say to you all at the start of the week? I said that I didn't want any messing around or stupid behaviour. Well, Northwood and Armstrong are both going back home on the train tonight and they'll be explaining themselves to the headmaster. What about you three? Have you been smoking? Have you been smoking drugs?'

'No Sir.'

'You, Stuart Seagrave. Have you been causing trouble again?'

'No Sir. Of course not Sir.'

'Turn out your pockets.'

'Sorry?'

'Empty your pockets. All three of you. Empty your pockets and show me what you've got in them.'

This is not good. The amplitude of Mr Gardner's rage has swept me into a state of trembling terror. I can feel myself shaking. We should be able to get through this though. As long as neither Martin nor Seagrave say or do anything stupid we might still get away with it. I can just make out Seagrave in my peripheral vision. He does not look good. Please don't be sick on the teacher, Seagrave. Being sick on the teacher would be very bad. Mr Gardner again demands us to turn out our pockets. Well at least there's nothing in any of my pockets that is going to get me into trouble. That's some small comfort. I slip my hands into my anorak pockets. In my left pocket is a stone. Oh yeah, the stone from the beach, with the writing on it, I'd forgotten about that. And in my right pocket I can feel a small, crumpled cardboard shape. A bit like a cigarette packet, only it isn't.

Oh Jesus...

Chapter 17

Here I am, creeping slowly up the hotel stairs in total darkness, one step at a time, cautiously moving up to the second floor. I'm going as fast as I dare, extra conscious of being seen or heard by anyone else, though my chest is pounding like never before. My feet feel their way up each carpeted step of the stairway until I'm at the top.

The second floor corridor stretches out ahead. The lights are out up here as well and I'm loath to turn them on. I feel my way along the wall. Carefully. The walls feel like they are covered with the same woodchip material used in my own room. I can't tell what colour it is in this gloom but I'm guessing it's the same dull beige that is the overall paint scheme of the hotel.

Gradually my eyes adjust to the half-light and I find my way along more easily. There are lights on inside some of the rooms which are showing under the doors. They make the edges of the carpet glow. I count off the brass numbers on each hotel room door as I go past, 23,

24, 25. Leena said that Jen is in room 29. The far end of the corridor.

When I get to 26 there's a slight change in level, a couple of steps go up before the corridor continues. I go up the first step and the floorboard creaks underneath me. I freeze for a moment on hearing the noise, then recompose and continue. 26, 27, 28.

I'm here. Room 29. I can see there's a light on inside. Here it is then. The moment that my racing heart has been building towards all day. Here I go. I rap on the door with a knock that I am hoping indicates both sensitivity and purposefulness.

There's movement on the other side of the door. The heavy, old door lock mechanism clunks and the door opens and there she is.

'Hello you,' she smiles.

'Hi.'

'Come in.'

I go in. Inside the room is the same as my own one, the same decoration and furniture. The same arrangement of double bed and bunk beds.

Jen's hair is loose, no longer tied in a ponytail. It partly covers one half of her face.

'How are you?' Jen asks me.

'Yes, good,' I say, looking at her. 'Actually I've been thinking about what you were telling me earlier. You know, that philosophy thing about whether the mind and the body are two, separate things. I've had an idea about that.'

'Okay,' She looks at me and smiles. 'Do you want to talk about that now? Or later?'

'Well if I can perhaps just tell it to you first. You know, while I still have it in my mind.'

'Okay then. What is it?'

'What?'

'What is it you want to say, Adam? What is it?'

'What is it?'

What is it?

No, no, no. This is all wrong. I'm sorry but I'm going to have to stop myself here. I have to level with you: the scene I've just described, creeping up to Jen's room and meeting her in there, it never happened. There have been many times in the last thirty-five years when I have gone back there in my mind, gone back to the Shore Haven Hotel and thought about how different things could have been if I had made it up to Room Twenty-Nine that night. But the actual truth is that I never did. I never made it to the room. I never got to see Jen.

When you are retelling some event from your past, some story from years ago, it's tempting to embellish it, to improve some parts of it, to add some bits or leave out others. It's easy to make it sound like you were a better and braver and generally a more interesting person than you really were. If there are things that you regret doing or are embarrassed about you can either change them, or leave them out entirely, or make them happen to one of the other characters. It turns out that if you want to make a better copy of yourself you don't need a computer as big as the Earth, all you need are the right words and a bit of imagination.

However, the problem is, once you start doing this it's easy to lose track of what was real – what actually happened compared to what you've subsequently made up. People do tell me that I have a good memory, but I can't help wondering just how much of what I think I remember did actually happen. Unlike Stuart Seagrave, I never kept a diary, so I don't have what historians call a primary source to confirm the truth. I've relived that field trip in my mind so often over the years. When it comes to the details, I'm no longer sure how much of it was real and how much is the product of my imagination.

But no, however tempting it is to embellish and improve on things, there comes a point when you have to draw a line. Like I said, I never did get to see Jen that night.

Here's what actually happened...

Chapter 17
(Second Attempt)

'Empty your pockets. Show me what you've got in them.'

Mr Gardner glowered at the three of us standing there before him. My body was ramrod-straight and I was too petrified to move. My heart was thumping and I could feel an icy bead of sweat running down my back, like meltwater from a mountain trickling down into some cold, dark, glacial pool. And all while the fingers in my anorak pocket were doing a dance of despair around the edges of the Durex packet.

'You. Martin Vickers.'

'Me, Sir?'

'Yes you, Sir. Show me what you've got in your pockets.'

I kept my eyes pointing straight ahead of me, like a soldier under inspection. To my left I could hear Martin fumbling with the buttons on the pockets of his flak jacket. The buttons must have been stiff as he was struggling to undo them. I had no idea what he had in those pockets or how long this whole process took. It was probably mere seconds but it felt like a geological age.

'What's that?' barked Mr Gardner.

From the corner of my eye I could see that Martin had something in his hand. Mr Gardner took it from him and examined it. Very slowly, I allowed my head to turn so I could see what it was. A tin of some kind. A small, flat, silver tin. A tobacco tin. What was Martin doing with that?

'You told me you hadn't been smoking.' Mr Gardner opened the tin and inspected its contents.

'I wasn't, Sir.'

'You've been smoking drugs with Northwood and Armstrong. Haven't you?'

'No, Sir...'

'You lied to me. You're a liar.'

'No, Sir...' Listening to him speak, it was as if the bold, brazen Martin Vickers had somehow fallen away and all that remained was this small, childlike voice.

'Get yourself in there with those two.' Mr Gardner jabbed a finger towards the entrance to the hotel bar, through which I could make out two shadowy shapes hunched inside.

'But Sir...'

'Hush up and get in there. I'll deal with you later.'

With leaden feet and a diminished posture, Martin shuffled off to where he had been told to go.

Mr Gardner glared at Seagrave and me. 'What about you two? Have you been smoking that stuff as well?'

'No, Sir.'

'Of course not, Sir.'

'You. Stuart Seagrave. Pockets.'

It seemed highly likely that Seagrave was going to suffer a total collapse at any moment. However drunk he had been beforehand, the drama of the current situation had caused him to sober up pretty sharpish. With shaking hands and a whimpering voice he showed Mr Gardner what he had in his pockets, which wasn't much, just some tissues, his suitcase key and a pencil.

'Right, Adam Gunson. Now you.'

Slowly, nervously, I pulled out the linings of the two pockets on either side of my anorak and showed him the contents.

'What's this?'

'It's a stone, Sir. We found it on the beach on Tuesday.'

Mr Gardner took the stone from me and studied it. 'It's got writing on it.'

'Yes, Sir.'

'"Principal Parts". What does that mean?'

'Don't know, Sir.'

'Principal parts of what?'

'Don't know, Sir.'

'Anything else in your pockets?'

'No, Sir.'

'Very well.' He passed the stone back to me. 'You two get yourselves back up to your room and stay there. I don't want to hear of any more trouble. You hear me?'

'Yes, Sir.'

Right, so you're going to want me to explain, aren't you? The whole time that these events were happening my fingers could not stop fidgeting in my anorak pocket. As well as nervously fiddling with the Durex packet they were also ferreting their way around the torn hole that had previously formed in the pocket lining. I don't know if it was a conscious move on my part or if it was pure instinct, I'm not sure how it happened but, all the while that Mr Gardner was interrogating the other two, my fingers were tearing at the hole, making it bigger, and scrunching up the Durex packet, making it smaller. And then, again seemingly by instinct, my fingers were pressing the screwed up cardboard through the hole. I remember feeling it drop through into the lining just as Mr Gardner turned his attention to me. And when he ordered me to show him the contents of my pockets I pulled out the linings of both pockets and was able to show him that the right side one was empty. I have no idea whether Mr Gardner saw the torn hole in the pocket lining or the damaged stitching. He didn't mention it if he had. All I knew was that, by some miracle, I had survived.

I followed Seagrave straight up the stairs and straight to the door of our room. From the lobby we could hear that the rest of the Tangley Wood students were now back from the pub, having been herded in by Mrs Lewis. A whole load more grief was about to go down.

'Unlock the door then,' said Seagrave.

'I don't have the key.'

'I don't have it either. Vickers must have it. Oh, terrific.'

We stood outside the room to our door for what seemed like eons, listening to the raging Gardner volcano as it peppered everyone in the lobby with a continuous hail of wrath. And then the shouting stopped and everyone started trudging up the stairs and heading towards their rooms. A few pairs of eyes looked in our direction but no one said anything. There were a few sniggers but mostly all the traces of merriment had been wiped away. Doors were unlocked and bodies disappeared into rooms and Seagrave and I were alone in the corridor once more.

'What was Vickers doing with tobacco?' Seagrave asked. 'I never saw him smoking.'

'He hangs out with Rob Northwood and that lot,' I replied. 'You see them sometimes smoking outside the school back gate. He was probably carrying it just to be sociable with them.'

'He didn't have any drugs though, did he? He only had the tobacco. And he wasn't even smoking it. Surely Mr Gardner can't send him home just for that?'

'You saw how Gardner was just now,' I said. 'I think that's just the way things were going.'

We now heard the sound of more anger from Mr Gardner. This time it was muffled so I'm guessing it was coming from the bar area that the three young offenders had been corralled into. We continued just standing there, not saying anything, not doing anything, trying to process what had just happened. Another ten minutes must have passed before Martin came up the stairs.

'They're sending us home,' he said as he unlocked the door. 'Rob, Paul and me. Gardner's gonna put us on a train and send us back to Woking.'

'What, tonight?'

'Yeah, there's a train leaving at eleven from Haverfordwest. Gardner's gonna drive us there now. I've just come to get my things.'

Martin started gathering up his stuff. There wasn't much to gather, just his underwear, his AC/DC tee shirt, his comics, some bits from the bathroom and the few scraps of paper that constituted his field trip work.

'What do you think will happen to you?' asked Seagrave as Martin crammed his belongings into his carrier bag. 'D'you think they'll expel you?'

'Probably,' said Martin. 'They'll probably tell me to leave the school, yeah.'

'God Vickers, I'm sorry. That is so unfair. Surely they can't send you home just because you had some tobacco on you. There must be some right of appeal.'

'Nah, bollocks to it,' said Martin. 'I'm done with that school. There's a better life for me out there.' With his bag packed Martin stood at the door facing Seagrave and me. 'Right then, you two tossers, I guess this is goodbye.' He turned to Seagrave and stared him straight in the eye, 'Remember what we talked about, yeah? Get your life sorted out, get yourself some better gear, make sure you get yourself to university and make sure you ask Roz to go out with you. Right?'

'Yes, right.'

And with that Martin Vickers, heavy metal music fan and would-be SAS commando, walked out the door and closed it behind him and was gone.

Seagrave and I sat there in silence for what seemed like ages. He was visibly shaken by the stress of it all and I was too. Yes, I had survived Mr Gardner's interrogation, yes, I had avoided him finding the Durex packet in my pocket, but there was no feeling of victory, no elation of having got away with it. The time was now twenty to nine. Way past when I was supposed to be meeting Jen in her room. And it still wasn't too late for me to go up there. But instead of going I just sat on the bunk bed, silently turning over in my mind everything that had just happened.

I wanted to leave the room, I wanted to go upstairs and see Jen, but what if I got caught? What if Mr Gardner or Mrs Lewis were stood at the end of the corridor, keeping guard? What if there were police downstairs interviewing the offenders? If I were to get caught there was a good chance that I would be placed on the next train out of Pembrokeshire as well.

But no, I couldn't leave things like that. I had to see Jen, even if it was just for a few minutes, or just a few seconds even. I had to go up to Jen's room. I had to be fearless and intrepid. The door wasn't locked, it was open to me. And I was going to walk through it.

'What the hell are you doing?' said Seagrave as I opened the door.

'I'm just popping out for a moment.' I stuck my head through the partly opened door and checked the corridor outside was empty.

'What? Are you mental? If Mr Gardner catches you he'll do his pieces.'

'I won't be long.' And before Seagrave could protest any further I slipped out the door and closed it behind me.

The stairs up to the second floor were at the end of the corridor. Slowly and cautiously I made my away past the lines of doors on either side. No sound was coming from any of the other rooms. I reached the end of the corridor, my chest pounding like never before. To my right, I could see the stairs that went on upwards to the second floor. To my left I could see the stairs that went down to the lobby and the hotel reception desk and –

'Adam Gunson! What do you think you're doing?' Stood in the lobby at the foot of the stairs were Mrs Lewis and the hotel manager. 'You were told to stay in your room. Get back there right now!'

'Sorry Miss.' I turned and sheepishly returned to where I had come from.

'You idiot!' said Seagrave as I re-entered the room. 'What did you think was going to happen?'

As I closed the door I saw the lights go off in the corridor.

Chapter 18

The mood the following morning was tense and awkward. A dark silence hung over us as we all gathered in the bar area before breakfast. Mr Gardner addressed the group and gave a terse summary of the previous night's events. He told us how Rob Northwood, Paul Armstrong and Martin Vickers had all been put on the train home last night. He also spoke about how each and every one of us had betrayed his trust by leaving the hotel yesterday evening when we had expressly been told not to. Mrs Lewis had discovered almost everyone rushing back from the direction of the Admiral Totty pub and, whilst it couldn't be proved that we had all been in there, the teachers were not going to let us take them for fools.

It wasn't practical to send all of us home, especially as today was the last day of the field trip. So instead we all stood there, staring at our shoes, while Mr Gardner continued to admonish us with the fiery intensity of a pyroclastic cloud.

I hadn't slept much during the night. I just had the same series of thoughts churning around in my head. I don't think Seagrave had slept that night either. He certainly wasn't making the kinds of noises he usually did when he was asleep. I just lay there, in-between the nylon sheets, thinking about all the things that had happened to me that day, but mostly thinking about Jen.

I had considered making another try at getting to her room. I thought about waiting until Seagrave was asleep and then creeping out of the room again, feeling my way along the dark corridor, finding my way up to Room Twenty-Nine. I thought about it then and I've thought about it many times since. But Seagrave didn't fall asleep, so far as I could tell. And, even if he had, I'm not so sure that I would have found the courage to try a second time. Jen had told me I was fearless and intrepid, but she had me all wrong. And so that was how the night had ended for me. I didn't manage to get to see Jen. And it was something that I have regretted ever since.

As a result of Mr Gardner's chastisements we were late getting into breakfast. I was nervous about entering the dining room and seeing Jen in there. She probably hated me for standing her up. Would she say anything when she saw me? I had no clear idea of what I was going to do. But when we got in there the Kimble College table was empty. They had had their breakfast and were already gone, with just the plates and cups and half-used miniature jam jars showing they had been there.

The activity for our final day was a map-reading exercise. We were to be driven out to some countryside location and from there we were to navigate our way back using an OS map and compass. As we stepped out into the car park I saw that the Kimble College minibus was all packed up and ready to move off. And there was Jen at one of the windows. On seeing her I felt a sense of joy but also panic. What would her expression be when she saw me? Would she hate me? Would she turn away in disgust?

But when she did see me she immediately shifted in her seat and smiled a big, bright, beaming smile. I have no idea what my face was doing but I think I was smiling back at her. I hope I was. Leena was sat behind her. She saw me too. She didn't smile. As the minibus started to move, Jen's lips were mouthing some words but I couldn't make out what they were. And she seemed to be pointing at something behind me. But then the minibus drove out of the car park and she was gone and that was the last time I ever saw her.

Mr Gardner had decided that things needed to be shaken up. Obviously the groups we had been working in had contributed to all the bad behaviour last night so he had split us up and put us into new ones. I was assigned to a group with Colin Winchester, Gemma Thorneycroft and Julie Whitworth. Colin took charge of the OS map and Gemma the compass. We were all driven out in the minibuses and dropped at different locations.

We had two hours to navigate our way back to the hotel. It was another fine morning with a clear blue sky and we found ourselves walking in some fine areas of country but, to be honest with you, my mood was so flat that I had very little inclination to join in. I just let Colin and Gemma do the navigating while I trailed along behind.

I think we must have gone astray a few times. At one point we came across a dead sheep at the side of a field. And further along we encountered a bunch of tin cans riddled with shot gun holes. These discoveries echoed the general miserableness that I think we were all feeling. At another point we had to climb over a style to reach the next field. Gemma did not manage this well and ended up face down in a puddle, her hair and jump suit soaked with farm slurry. Such a scene would normally have enticed some hilarity but none of us were really in the mood. We managed to get ourselves back to the hotel within the two hour limit without any further drama.

The afternoon was allocated as free time. I don't recall much of what I did in detail. A few of us went into the games room for a bit and played pool or had a go on the consoles. I just wandered around the beach front trying to fill in the time as best I could. I walked along the road, up the shops to where the pub was and back again. There weren't any other people about. I sat myself down on the iron bench next to the Cocktail Club and stared out towards the horizon. I thought about going down onto the beach and out towards the sea. It looked inviting but it was also full of that black mud and I didn't want to be walking in that.

I couldn't listen to the Walkman any more: the batteries had died and I didn't have any money to buy new ones. So I just sat there for I'm not sure how long, with thoughts of everything that had happened to me rolling about inside my head. And then I became aware that a shadow had formed on the bench next to me. What could this be, I wondered. Could it be that some godlike alien being from the planet Jupiter had come down from the sky and was going to make everything okay? No, of course it wasn't that. It was Isaac.

'Alright?' he said, sitting down beside me.

'Alright,' I murmured in reply

'Hey, I never finished telling you about my discovery.'

'What?'

'You know, what I was telling you last night. The blast furnace diagram. Why the teachers keep getting us to draw the same diagram all the time. There's obviously some kind of conspiracy. There's obviously some reason for our minds being manipulated in this way. But the question is, why? The image must mean something. But what? What does it mean? And then it suddenly came to me.' Isaac's eyes were almost dancing with excitement, as if he had chanced upon some secret truth about the universe. His voice slipped down to a whisper as he continued. 'It's a message.'

'A message?'

'Yeah.'

'What kind of message?' I don't know why I asked but I asked anyway.

'From another world, obviously. A message from aliens from another planet. They've somehow managed to get this image into all the school books and lessons in all the schools so they can communicate with the children of Earth. It's so obvious, I can't believe I hadn't realised it before. All this time I've been spending looking at the sky for the signs of alien life when it's actually been here the whole time. Right in front of me.'

I turned my head and looked at him. 'Okay, so let me get this right. What you're saying is that beings from another world have been secretly communicating with us by putting messages in our school text books?'

'Correct.'

'Isaac?'

'Yes?'

'Will you please just piss off.'

Chapter 19

The Tangley Wood School music room was on the far side of the complex, next to the science block and opposite the dining hall. I had waited until three thirty, the end of the school day, before heading over there. It was the Tuesday after we had all returned from the geography field trip. The school summer term had started while we had been away. I had neglected to tell my other teachers that I was going to miss the first two days of the new term, which had got me into a little bit of trouble. But I didn't particularly care.

There was no one else in the music room when I arrived. Usually it would be a hive of activity with boys and girls coming to and from various music lessons, collecting instruments or returning them to the store cupboard. But not today, I had the room to myself.

I waited there a few minutes, slouched against the timpani drums that lived under the window, a position that gave me a good view of all the comings and goings outside. And then through the window I saw Roz. She was walking along the pavement that ran alongside the science block. My eyes followed her as she moved closer, her book-filled school bag hanging awkwardly off her left shoulder. I knew that she would be coming in here; there had been the usual orchestra practice at lunchtime and she would stop by to collect her piccolo.

She came in through the door. 'Oh, hi,' she said, spotting me.

'Hello,' I replied. In all the time I had known her there had probably never been more than half a dozen words shared between us. This would prove to be one of our longer conversations.

'What are you doing here?'

I've come to see you Roz. To ask you if you would like to go out with me. Was what I had gone there with the full intention of saying to her. But I didn't say that. Instead I said that I was waiting for Derek Hotchkiss, that I'd agreed to meet him there as he had some new tapes for me.

'Oh, right,' said Roz as she retrieved her piccolo from the cupboard. 'Bye then.' And then she walked out the door and was gone.

When I had got back from the field trip I had cycled over to Derek's house and had told him what had happened. I didn't tell him everything. I told him about the daily activities and my miserable sleeping arrangements and the bad business that had led to Martin and the others being sent home. But I didn't tell him about Jen. I thought about telling him but I decided not to. The time I spent with Jen was something that I was going to keep just for me. But I did tell him that I hadn't managed to do the thing I had promised to do, namely, asking Roz to go out with me. Because Roz hadn't been there.

Derek told me what he had learnt in my absence. The reason why Roz hadn't gone on the field trip. Apparently the company her dad worked for had offered him a new job, a promotion, but it required him to relocate to Australia. The whole family were going to move out there. Roz had missed the field trip because she and her family had been out in Melbourne taking a look at their new home. She was back in Britain now and back at the school but only for a few more weeks. And then she would be moving out to Australia for good.

So if I was going to ask her out it needed to be now, or else it would in every sense be too late. Hence Derek had pressured me to kick on with it. Hence why I had been waiting in the music room for Roz.

But when the moment arrived, I didn't ask her. And the reason I didn't ask her was a very simple one. I could tell you that it was because she was going away and it was never going to work and all that kind of thing. But no, the reason that in the end I didn't ask her was because, apparently, I wasn't in love with her anymore. And as I wasn't in love with her there seemed no point in doing it.

It was a strange thing, being in love with Roz. About two months ago it had just happened to me, it had seemed to come out of nowhere and it was the most amazing feeling I had ever known. And then, just as suddenly, it was gone. Somewhere between a Space Invaders game and a derelict beach bar, my feelings for Roz Madsen had just disappeared. And a few weeks later Roz was gone too. Gone from the school, gone from the country, gone from my life and gone from my world without ever having really been in it.

So that was it. That was the story of the geography field trip. It had started badly and it had ended badly but there had been a bit in the middle that had been absolutely brilliant.

The fallout from it all continued to be felt for some weeks afterwards. Rob Northwood, Paul Armstrong and Martin Vickers were all forced to leave the school and, like Roz, I was never to see any of them again. I had no regrets about Rob Northwood or Paul Armstrong; the school playground was arguably a far safer place without them in it. But I was less happy about what had happened to Martin. I'd been doubtful about sharing a room with him, given our previous history, it's true, but he didn't deserve the fate that had befallen him. Surely having a tin of tobacco in your pocket wasn't enough to warrant you being expelled, was it? But then it had been clear that Mr Gardner was in no mood for justice that night. Martin had said that he wanted to go out and find trouble and stare it in the face; he had certainly done that all right.

I didn't see much of Stuart Seagrave either in the days that followed. I'm also guessing that he hadn't asked Roz out either, as if he had I would surely have heard about it. What was noticeable, though, was that as the weeks of the new term progressed there was a visible change in Seagrave. Seemingly he had taken Martin's parting advice about improving his image.

Whenever I now saw him he appeared to be fitting in more, rather than standing out from the crowd. And on the odd occasion that I saw him outside school he had swapped those dreadful polyester trousers for something far more stylish. One time I even glimpsed him with a pair of Dunlop Green Flash trainers on his feet. But we didn't share any lessons and he seldom came into the sixth form common room so, aside from the weekly assembly, our paths rarely crossed. As the summer term moved on I saw less and less of Seagrave and, when the new school year started in September, it appeared that he too had left and gone elsewhere.

In the days and weeks after the field trip I found myself still thinking about Jen and those times I had spent with her. And it wasn't just because Jen was the first girl who had ever kissed me (although that did have some bearing on things, obviously). But no, I was thinking about those conversations we'd had, all the things she'd said she wanted to know about. Consciousness and the soul and the human mind. The things that make us what we are. Where does it all come from? Where do *we* come from? Jen wanted to find out if there were answers to those questions. And I came to realise that I wanted to know that as well.

During my time at school I had sat through a multitude of subjects and lessons and I'd never found any of them very engaging. But, for some reason, this 'philosophy' thing that Jen had told me about seemed to be different. I was curious about that in a way that I'd never been curious about anything before. Plus there was that big idea that had come to me during the minibus ride. That thing about whether the duplicate me would have the same mind, the same consciousness as the original me . Was that a real thing? A real piece of philosophy? It was still bugging me. Had anyone asked that question before? And if they had, what was the answer?

I tried talking it through with Derek round at his house one Saturday. But I don't think he properly grasped what I was getting at. He kept repeating that the duplicate of me would have its own mind and, yes, I know that, but the point I was trying to make was that it wouldn't be *my* mind. Maybe I hadn't explained myself too well. Derek dismissed it, telling me I was wasting my time. No, Derek was no help at all. But was there anything else I could do to try and find out the truth?

Eventually I ended up doing something I had never done before. I went to the school library. I had been in the school library before, but only for private study lessons. I'd never been in there to, you know, borrow a book.

Miss Howell, the school librarian, asked me what I was after and I said books on philosophy. She looked at me very doubtfully but directed me to a small cluster of shelves in one of the corners. The philosophy section of the Tangley Wood School library was neither well stocked nor well utilised. There were books on Socrates and Aristotle and a copy of Plato's *Phaedrus*. There was also a book by René Descartes. I remembered Jen had mentioned him as being important.

Miss Howell was astonished that I wanted to check out Descartes' *Meditations on First Philosophy.* But she stamped my brand new library card for me anyway and I took the book away, excitedly thinking that this might tell me the solution. But I just couldn't get on with it. I tried reading it but nothing would sink in. The writing was so dense, so hard to understand that I gave up before I had even finished the first ten pages.

The library had another book that claimed to be 'an Introduction to Western Philosophy'. That book, whilst it was at least aimed at the right reading age for me, didn't seem to help me much either. If anything, it gave me more questions than it did answers.

Was there anyone else I could talk to? Tangley Wood didn't offer philosophy as an O Level or A Level subject so there were no teachers I could ask. With no immediate help at hand I began to come to the conclusion that, if I was ever going to find out the truth, I would need to get more serious. I would need to get serious about philosophy. And so it was that, one morning in June, I was doing another thing I had never in all my life thought I would ever do. I was sitting in the careers office having a discussion with Mrs Lewis, in her capacity as careers teacher.

The careers department of Tangley Wood School had never received much in the way of investment. It comprised a small, solitary room below the stairwell of the home economics block. And it was in this tiny room that I now sat, with Mrs Lewis opposite and a narrow, cluttered desk in-between us. It was plain to me from the start that she viewed my presence there with suspicion. Doubtless she remembered me as being one of the primary offenders from the field trip.

'So, Adam, you want to study philosophy?'

'Yes Miss. At Bath University, if possible.'

'Bath? Why Bath in particular?'

'I heard that they have a really good philosophy course there.'

'Well you've never shown any interest in further education before. Where's all this come from?'

'I met someone who was doing philosophy and what they told me made me want to learn more about it. Stuff about the human mind, consciousness, where it comes from, what makes us who we are. That kind of thing.'

'I see,' she said, doubtfully.

Here in her personal realm, her natural habitat, Mrs Lewis was assertive, questioning, challenging. I considered furthering my cause by telling her about my big philosophical idea, but decided against it.

Mrs Lewis continued to probe me while referring to some brochures that were spread out on her desk. 'What A Level subjects are you doing?'

'Maths, chemistry and geography.'

'Are you not doing English?'

'Err, no.'

'I see. Well I'm sorry, Adam,' she went on, 'but all the philosophy courses here have A Level English Language as a minimum requirement. You should have expressed your interest in philosophy earlier, when you were making your A Level choices. There's nothing we can do about that now. My advice is that you focus on the A Levels that you are actually doing and put other distractions out of your mind. If you are genuinely interested in going onto further education we can look at what courses and colleges might be suitable for you...'

It's strange, the way that time appears to move at different speeds during different periods of your life. When you're a child the years move by very slowly – the length of time between one Christmas and the next seems absolutely massive. But as you get older the years pass so much faster. I've come across a couple of explanations as to why this is the case. One possible reason is that, when you are a child, a single year seems such a long time because it represents such a big proportion of your life so far. Another is that, when you are young, every day is full of new experiences. But as you get older you start doing more of the same things each day and time seems to pass more slowly when you are doing new and different stuff.

On balance, I tend to favour the second of these explanations. It certainly accounts for why I can recall the events of the field trip so clearly. That time was full of new experiences: it was the first time I had been away from home without my parents; the first time I'd shared a hotel room with two other boys; the first time I'd ever met anyone like Jen. Everything about those five days was different. In contrast, I don't remember the weeks that followed anything like as clearly.

Towards the end of that summer I had a mighty bust-up with Derek. I had borrowed his Walkman again and he had accused me of breaking it after it chewed up his copy of *The Unforgettable Fire*. He also told me that he resented making all those music tapes for me when I hadn't done any for him in return, And I, in response, had a go at him for seemingly not being capable of understanding my big philosophical idea. And he said that there was no point in trying to understand it because it didn't pass the 'stupid' test. The outcome was that we had had a big falling-out. Also, Derek had managed to find himself a girlfriend. He was now spending his time with her and had stopped inviting me round at weekends. So we no longer hung out together as much as we used to. When our time at Tangley Wood came to an end Derek went on to do a Maths degree at Loughborough. And from then on we sort of lost touch.

* * *

Unlike Derek, I didn't go to university or polytechnic. I just coasted through my remaining time in the sixth form, much as I had done before. I took my final exams and left with some fairly average A Level results.

My mum and dad were less than impressed with my efforts. They told me that, if I wasn't going to university, then I had to find work and start paying my way. I had no real enthusiasm to join the ranks of the employed but, propelled by my father's firm words, I searched in the local paper and reluctantly put in applications for a few different jobs. One of these was for a starting position at the Woking branch of the Mid-Westland Bank and, after doing the interview (and much to my surprise), they decided to take me on.

It turned out that a few of us from Tangley Wood had also got jobs there, including Chas Browning and Gemma Thorneycroft. The work they gave us to do was stunningly dull but it was easy and at least it was nice to be alongside some familiar faces.

Somehow Gemma and I even ended up going out together for a while. She even let me drive her Escort XR3 a couple of times (it turned out that it wasn't actually that nice to drive). But Gemma and I didn't really have that much in common. For one thing, she didn't like Phil Collins. I managed to get tickets to the Genesis concert at Wembley Stadium but she didn't want to go to it; apparently Rachel Barrett had some tickets to the London premier of *The Living Daylights* which was on the same night and she wanted to go to that instead.

Can you believe that? So no, there was never going to be anything long term between us.

And then one lunch time, shortly after the Genesis concert, I happened to be sat in the office rest room, idly flicking through some magazines that had been left on one of the coffee tables. Among them was an Open University brochure for adult education courses. And one of the courses caught my eye. It was called 'Philosophy and the Mind'. The course was in the form of home learning with evening classes. And it got me thinking again about that big philosophical idea of mine. The title of the course implied that it might be interesting. Maybe doing this course might enable me to finally discover the truth about all that.

There were no necessary qualifications required to do the course. No need for you to have already passed A Level English or anything similar (that's why it's called the 'Open' University). There was one catch, though. 'Philosophy and the Mind' was a level two course. I couldn't do that course without doing the associated level one course first. The level one course was called 'Humanities: A Foundation'. What was a 'humanity'? I had no idea. But, according to the description, this course covered a basic grounding in philosophy as well as other stuff including French history, twentieth century art, the Metaphysical Poets and Jacobean drama.

Anyway I thought I'd give it a go, so I signed up for the foundation course. Purely, you understand, so I could get onto the 'Philosophy and the Mind' course later. I had my doubts about going back to education so soon after leaving school, but I did it anyway. And you know what? I was wrong to have doubts. Because it was nothing like being at school. The tutorials were totally different to all the lessons I had sat through at Tangley Wood. The tutorials were genuinely interesting.

I stuck with it and the weeks went by and, little by little, lesson by lesson, I actually started to learn something about philosophy. All those complex ideas about valid arguments and sound arguments and formal fallacies and begging the question; once the tutor had explained them I actually began to understand that stuff. And once I understood it, it became enjoyable. And engaging. And for the first time in ages I felt like I was somewhere where I wanted to be. I felt like I was somewhere where I... belonged.

(It was during this period of my life that I was also briefly involved with an art rock band called The Cuban Missiles. But that's a whole other story for another time.)

By the time of my second year, when I was part-way through the 'Philosophy and the Mind' course, I was becoming confident in the subject. Confident to the point where I regularly found myself helping some of my fellow students, explaining parts of the course that they were struggling with. And my tutor, noticing how I was doing this and the way I was explaining things, asked me whether I had ever considered a career in teaching. Which I hadn't. But then again, I had been starting to question whether that job at the bank was right for me. The time I'd spent in those evening classes was making me think there could be more to life than pushing bank statements into envelopes and filing cheque books in alphabetical order. Maybe there was another door that I could walk through instead.

So that's what I did. That's the choice I made. And it's a choice that has ultimately brought me to the place where I am right now, thirty-odd years later, sat in front of a college laptop and struggling to mark a bunch of essays about Isaiah Berlin. Most people I know would tell you that my route to here began when I first picked up a philosophy book. Or when I started that Open University course. Or when my old philosophy teacher suggested that I think about a career in teaching. But it had really all begun during the geography field trip. It had begun with Jen: Jen beating me at Space Invaders; Jen eating biscuits while telling me about René Descartes; Jen kissing me in a busted-up building on the sea front; Jen who wasn't Jennifer and wasn't Jenny or even Jenna, just Jen.

Chapter 20

Why do people keep going on about passion? Because we need to. We all need to have something in our lives. Something that gives them meaning. Something that makes them worthwhile. Like my colleague Tim Brenner, English teacher and supporter of Cove Alexandra Football Club. It's not about whether his team wins or loses, it's about having something to belong to, something to be part of. We all need things like that. We all need passions.

But they do need to be the right kind of passions. And sitting here trying to relive things that happened thirty-five years ago is probably not the best thing to be doing, is it? A passion may be something that happens to you, something you don't choose, something you don't have full control over, but that doesn't mean you have to be a slave to it. If you employ a bit of positive freedom you can keep your passions in check.

I still haven't made much progress with those essays. I should have made more of an effort sooner instead of wasting my time looking at Facebook and dwelling on the past. To be fair though, most of the essays I have read so far have been quite well written. They show a solid level of work and a good understanding of the topic. Normally I would have had the chance to meet my new students face to face in a tutorial, before receiving their first written work. But then again, we're all living in challenging times right now, aren't we?

I don't think I'll be going to the Tangley Wood School reunion. I'm not sure it would be such a good idea. I keep looking at that photo. The one showing the sixth form common room at Christmas. The walls and ceiling are all dressed in balloons and paper chains. And there we all are, lined up for the camera, some of us in fancy dress and others in their pantomime costumes. Derek and Gemma and Julie and Chas and Rachel... all those young faces. But of course they'll all be different now. They'll all have moved on with their lives. Just looking at their Facebook profiles has shown me evidence enough of that.

The first profile I looked at was Derek's. He's now married to his second wife, has two children, works as a sales manager at an insurance firm and apparently has visited six percent of the world's countries. He's also lost most of his hair in the intervening years. Like I said, I lost contact with Derek after he went off to university. He was my best and oldest friend, though. I should have made more of an effort to stay in touch with him. That's another thing that I regret not doing.

Chas Browning and Colin Winchester are both also married with families, as are Julie and Rachel and most of the others. None of them appear to be living in the Woking area any more.

Martin Vickers is not showing as a member of the group but Colin has mentioned that he heard about him some time back. Apparently Martin did join the army and later served in the First Gulf War. While in Iraq he got caught up in a friendly fire incident and was seemingly responsible for saving several lives. It sounds like that Plan B of his may have worked out for him after all.

There's no sign of Stuart Seagrave anywhere, although one of the others seems to think that he ended up working in financial services. Rob Northwood is there though. He's posted a message saying, 'What, am I the only one of us who's spent time in prison?'

Probably the most surprising of all is Isaac. It looks like he kept going with all that UFO and conspiracy stuff as he now has his own YouTube channel devoted to it: 'The Mysterious World of Isaac Lee – Strange and Bizarre True Stories from the Master of the Unexplained'. The whole thing sounds like a load of nonsense to me, same as it always did. I tried watching one of his videos earlier. Isaac doesn't appear on screen, you just get his voice talking over film clips and going on about subjects like crystal skulls, crop circles and the secret rulers of the world. His voice is still the same, nasally, monotone drone that it was back at school. Two minutes of listening to that was enough for me. But apparently there are people out there who are really into this stuff. He has more than a hundred thousand subscribers and his videos get millions of views. His channel is sponsored by health food drinks and VPN tools. I think that Isaac has become what they call an 'influencer'.

And then there's Roz, of course. There she is, her profile picture gazing back at me in a way she never did in real life. She had stayed out in Australia for a number of years but is now back, married with three children and living in York, apparently. Would it do me any good to see her again? Probably not. The Roz I used to think about doesn't exist now and probably didn't exist then either. I haven't really thought about her that much since then, which is surprising, seeing as how she was the original love of my life.

So no, I don't think I'll be going to the school reunion. I can't keep raking over the past. It's better to just leave it all alone. I've sent a response back to Julie and told her I won't be going.

I do still have one souvenir from the geography field trip – that stone I found on the beach. It lives in that random box of stuff I keep in the cupboard under the stairs. The writing on it, 'Principal Parts' is still just about legible but the felt pen ink has faded with time. I've showed the stone to a number of people over the years to try and unlock what it means. The general responses I've had are that the writing on the stone represents some bad thing, some horrible memory.

Something that, for whatever reason, the person who wrote it wanted to forget. So they had written the words on the stone and thrown it from the top of the cliff into the sea. They were literally throwing the memory out of their life.

That explanation seems to make sense. But the meaning of the words 'principal parts' is something that I've struggled to find a decent answer to. The best I've heard so far came from one of my old Open University colleagues. He had been privately educated and had told me that 'principal parts' were something you did in Latin classes at prep school. In short, the principal parts of a Latin verb are a summary of all its different variations. He said that there were whole lists of these principal parts that you needed to learn for the common entrance exams to public schools and trying to master them all was a very tiresome business. So maybe some unhappy Latin student, thoroughly miserable after trying to learn all the principal parts of Latin verbs, had written those words onto the stone and tossed it off the cliff. I know, it sounds like a bit of a thin story, but it's the best that I've managed to find so far.

Oh, and of course there was also my big philosophical idea. That thing I had hoped to impress Jen with. I suppose that was a sort of a take-away from the field trip. I spent ages over the years trying to figure out the truth about that. I even made it the subject of my PhD. Sometimes I've even set my students an essay question based on that notion: if you were able to make an exact duplicate of yourself would that duplicate copy have the same mind, the same consciousness as you? And if it didn't, what would the implications be?

I've discussed it with many people over the years. Most, like Derek, didn't get it at all. Others, like my original philosophy tutor, felt I should focus more on neuroscience and materialist accounts of the mind, or try looking into alternative approaches like epiphenomenalism or panprotopsychism. One of my students a few years back gave an interesting answer; she said that you can't really think of the two bodies as being exact duplicates because they don't occupy the same area of space. For example, if you had two identical objects and shone a light on them, the two objects would each cast their own shadow. They wouldn't cast the same shadow. Her suggestion was that maybe human consciousness is sort of like a shadow cast by the brain.

But here's the thing that settled it for me. I had started out believing that the two duplicate copies of the person would be absolutely identical in material terms, because all the various different types of atoms and subatomic particles in the universe are identical. Well, it turns out that's not right. Apparently every electron in the universe has its own, unique energy value. It's that sodding Mr Charlton again! He's the one who told me that all atoms of the same type were identical, but it isn't true. He's the one whose teaching led me down that futile rabbit hole. Years after I last had a lesson with him and the guy was still messing up my life. Because, of course if the two duplicate copies, the two Captain Kirks or whatever, are not one hundred percent identical then the theory doesn't work. Kick away the initial premise of an argument and the rest will quickly come tumbling down with it.

I wonder if she remembers me. I certainly remember her. And sometimes I see her as well. Well no, I don't mean that I actually see her, I just see someone who reminds me of her, a face that looks like hers, a photo in a magazine or someone on TV who resembles her a bit. Last year I was in the Lenbachhaus art gallery in Munich, just wandering through and suddenly there she was, in a side room just off the main exhibition space, smiling back at me from one of the paintings. It wasn't actually *her*, obviously, as the information card said the picture had been painted by Franz Marc in 1910. But it looked so like her.

I did actually try and contact her in the months following the field trip. I managed to find an address for Kimble College in the school library and I wrote her a letter. I've never been much of a letter writer so it was a rather unstructured, rambling sort of letter. And I'm not sure what my expectations were or what I thought would come of it. But I at least wanted to explain what had happened that night and why I didn't manage to meet up with her. The problem was, though, that I never did know her full name. She had told me to call her Jen but I suspect that wasn't her actual first name. And of course I never knew her last name either. So the only name and address I could write on the envelope was Jen, Kimble College, Warrington. I'm guessing that it never got to her. I certainly never had a reply.

I wonder if she ever made it to Bath University, like she wanted. And I wonder what she did with her life. Hey, don't get me wrong. It's not like I think about her every day. No, sometimes whole months will pass. And there have been other women in my life. But still I often wonder where she is now and what she's doing. Not that there's any likelihood of me finding her, of course. Not now. Not after all this time. I mean, Facebook is all very well and good for finding and connecting people but the minimum information you need is the other person's name. And it's not as if –

Hang on.

Hang on a minute.

What about this for a thought? Julie set up the Facebook group for the Tangley Wood sixth form and put all of us into it as members. Might there be a similar Facebook group for Jen's college? And if there is, might she be a member? Hey, it's got to be worth a try, hasn't it?

The next thing I know, I'm typing the words 'Kimble College' into the Facebook search field. A whole list of possible options spring up on the screen. Kimble College Rugby Club Old Boys. Kimble College Old Kimbleens Association, Kimble College Gilbert and Sullivan Society... Hey, what about this one – Kimble College Graduates 1986? That sounds promising. I click through the series of links that leads to the list of group members and then watch as the screen fills up with pictures of various middle-aged people. I'm starting to get excited. I can feel my heart racing like a sixteen-year-old. There are over two hundred members of this thing, though. I start scrolling down the page.

Hey, that one looks a bit like Jen's friend, Leena. Same straight hair, same pallid complexion, same miserable look on her face. She's wearing a gold choker necklace and seems to be the HR director of some corporate thing. The name on the profile isn't Leena though so I'm guessing it isn't her.

I continue sifting through the rows and rows of faces. Am I going to find her here? Seriously, what are the chances? How likely is it that I'm going to find her amongst this lot after all this time? Some of the people in here don't even have proper profile pictures. They have photos of children or pets. Why do people do that? It's so annoying. How are you supposed to know that you've found the right person on Facebook when their profile photo is a picture of a gerbil? Oh, why am I still wasting my time on this craziness? I mean, you have to agree, it's really doubtful that –

Just a minute. What about that one?

That one there?

I click on the picture and open the Facebook profile. That could be her. She looks a little different to how I remember her. But then again she's older, obviously. But it could be her. And she's even got her hair in a similar style to how it was back then. The photo appears to have been taken during a scuba-diving holiday somewhere in the Caribbean. It really looks like it could be her. But according to the profile her name isn't Jen, it's...

Wow! I never thought of *that*. Why did I never think of *that*?

But is it her? It might be. I mean, look at the photo. Look at that smile. It's unmistakable, isn't it? It's the same smile that smiled back at me from the door of the cocktail club as she was leaving. It's the same smile that smiled back at me from the window of the minibus as it was driving away. I'd recognise that smile anywhere. You could restart the sun with that smile.

Oh my God! Is it really her? Have I found her?

After all this time, have I actually found her?

What do I do? Should I try contacting her? That 'send message' button next to her picture is taunting me to click on it. But will she want to hear from me after all this time? Will she even remember me? Will she think it a bit weird that someone she only met briefly thirty-five years ago is now wanting to get in touch with her?

What do I do?

A notification flashes up in the bottom right corner of my laptop screen. It's an email telling me I have a new Facebook message. It's a message from Julie.

From: Julie Stonor
Hi Adam. No!!! Are you sure you can't come to the reunion? ☹☹ We need you there! You're the only one of us who seems to remember all the things that happened back then. It won't be the same without you being there. Please say you'll come? Please? Julie ☺☺☺ xxx

Now that's unexpected. Julie wants me to come because she thinks I remember things that others don't. Well, I suppose it's always nice when people tell you that you're wanted. And it's nice that she thinks I remember so much about all that happened back in those days. But I can't help wondering, on top of everything else, how much of it all do I really, actually, properly remember?

Neuroscience tells us that whenever you recall a memory you are actually using your imagination to visualise it, and doing that causes you to remake the memory every time. So every time you do that you are putting a little distance between the way you remember it and the way it really happened. And of course it doesn't really help if you spend loads of time reliving things in your imagination the way you wish they were, rather than the way they actually were. Do too much of that and you can start to lose track of reality. Like I said before, you may think that you can remember things from the past but it isn't necessarily true that you remember them correctly.

Julie is certainly keen on emojis, isn't she? This new message from her is once again liberally peppered with them. Like I said, I've never been one for emojis myself; Call me old-fashioned but I've always thought the English language was rich enough to not really need them. But then again, it has to be admitted that certain things cannot be conveyed using language alone.

Maybe I was too hasty in deciding not to go to the reunion. Maybe I should go. It might be fun to see everyone again. And I guess it would be kind of nice to see Derek. I do still regret that we didn't keep in touch. Yes, I think I'll go back to the woman formerly known as Julie Whitworth and tell her I've changed my mind.

And what about the woman who might once have been Jen? Should I try to contact her as well? What do you think? I feel like I should. I've no clear idea what I'm going to say to her. But I should be able to think of something.

It's strange, isn't it? I've been stuck in the house for the last couple of days basically doing nothing and yet, somehow, it feels as if an awful lot has happened.

You know what? I just can't concentrate on these essays right now. I'm going to leave the rest of them until later. I've spent too much time sat here staring at this laptop screen. I need to go and do something else.

What shall I do? Watch one of those films I had recorded, maybe? No, here's a better idea. How about sticking some music on? Yes, of course. I should have done this right at the start. This is a much better way to visit the past. Listening to old music will swoop you straight back to a time and place in a way that turning over memories in your mind never can.

What shall it be then? There's only one choice, isn't there? *No Jacket Required* by Phil Collins. That album has always been one of my favourites. I've bought it multiple times over the years – tape, vinyl album, CD, MP3 download. But I still have that copy Derek made for me. Yes, I know that it's worn out and one of the tracks is missing and the tape is twisted at one point. But there's something special about listening to that particular copy. The cassette case even has some sand in it from where I dropped it in the Milford Haven car park. I dig it out from the back of the desk drawer and hold it in my hand and look at it. That's my time machine, right there.

I pop it into the tape player and get it playing. Those first bass notes of 'Sussudio' start filling up the room and I'm instantly transported away to a brilliant place. I know Phil Collins has had his critics over the years and his music hasn't always been in fashion. But he really has done some great tunes and he's at his absolute best on this album. For those of you who have any doubts, my advice is that you get hold of a copy of *No Jacket Required* and listen to it four times uninterrupted.

If you still don't like Phil Collins after that then, well, I'm sorry but there's probably no hope for you. :-)

Acknowledgements

If you've made it as far as this page then I'm guessing you managed to get through the novel. If that is the case then thank you for reading it and I hope you found it moderately entertaining.

I first started trying to write what would ultimately become this novel back in 1986. I originally planned it as a contemporary school story but in its final form it has ended up as more of a period piece, a memento of the 1980s if you like.

There are a number of people I need to thank for their help. Special thanks must go firstly to my good friends Graham Smith and Steve Good. This project had been languishing unfinished for years and it's due to Graham's motivation that I actually pressed on and got the thing completed. Graham also allowed me to incorporate a couple of his ideas into the story. And thanks to Steve for giving me feedback and encouragement on an early draft and for kindly letting me feature the name of the football team he used to run, Cove Alexandra.

Thanks also to Fred Martin for extending the benefit of his knowledge and experience as an actual geography teacher and for guiding me on some of the technical aspects of a 1980s field trip.

Thanks to all of you who took the time to read early copies of the novel and provide me with feedback, suggestions and encouragement. Namely, Angela Price, Anna Molesworth, Gill Elliott, Carolyn Fields and Louise Smith. And thanks to Angela Johnson for giving me both her feedback and the benefit of her reviewing skills. All of your comments and suggestions have, I am confident, made the whole thing substantially better.

And lastly, a massive amount of thanks goes to my wife Helen for putting up with me while I was spending so much time and effort working on this crazy thing.

Love to you all.

Lol.

Bibliography

Berlin, I, *Two concepts of liberty: An inaugural lecture delivered before the University of Oxford, on 31 October 1958*, Oxford, Clarendon Press (1961)

Marx, K, Engels, F (2004), *The German Ideology*, London, Lawrence & Wishart Ltd

Warburton, N. (1999) *Arguments For Freedom*, Open University

Wilkinson, R. (1999) *Minds and Bodies*, Open University

Warburton, N, Pike, J, Matravers, D (2006), *Reading Political Philosophy*, Abingdon, Routledge/Open University

Frankish, K. (2005) *Consciousness*, Open University

Extract from *The Rubaiyat of Omar Khayyam* translated by Edward Fitzgerald (1859)

Sohrab and Rustum by Matthew Arnold (1853)

About the Author

Lol Watson was born in Epping in 1968. He grew up and spent most of his life living in Surrey and Hampshire, where he experienced education in both private and state schools. After leaving sixth form college he spent the next 35 years working in the financial services industry. In 2009 he completed an honours degree in philosophy and English literature from the Open University. He currently lives in Marlborough with his wife Helen. His passions include reading, writing, philosophy, enjoying the Wiltshire countryside and building Airfix model kits (of which he currently has far more than he can possibly ever complete). *The Positive Freedom Field Trip* is his first novel.

Printed in Great Britain
by Amazon